# DEATH IN THE MIST

BOOK 11 IN THE DI GILES SERIES

ANNA-MARIE MORGAN

## ALSO BY ANNA-MARIE MORGAN

In the DI Giles Series:

Book 1 - Death Master

Book 2 - You Will Die

Book 3 - Total Wipeout

Book 4 - Deep Cut

Book 5 - The Pusher

Book 6 - Gone

Book 7 - Bone Dancer

Book 8 - Blood Lost

Book 9 - Angel of Death

Book 10 - Death in the Air

DEATH IN THE MIST

Copyright © 2020 by Anna-marie Morgan
All rights reserved.

No part of this book may be reproduced in any form or by any electronic or mechanical means, including information storage and retrieval systems, without written permission from the author, except for the use of brief quotations in a book review.

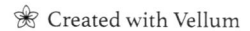

❦ Created with Vellum

*For my readers*

# 1

## DEATH IN THE SHADOWS

The mist rolled in, curling vaporous tentacles around street corners, filling the town before midnight.

A lone female meandered through it, trying to walk a straight line and failing. Hiccoughing misty clouds of alcohol-filled breath. Not for the first time, Alice wished she had worn more than a thin dress and a short jacket. A night like this needed a long, thick coat. Something she could sink into.

A paver clunked behind. Someone was following.

Spinning round, no-one was there. She breathed again. No problem. She just had to get home before falling to the gutter.

Not for the first time, she regretted leaving her friends to do this on her own, turning down their offer of a joint taxi home. Waiting required too much effort after a few drinks. Faster to walk. She knew it wasn't good to walk home alone, but didn't fancy a cold queue on a dank street.

Anyway, walking was good for you. She'd done it before;

she would do it again. Females in every town across the country would repeat this risky behaviour. And why not? Why shouldn't a woman be able to walk home whatever time she wanted to? It was a free country, wasn't it?

Footsteps.

A quick look round.

Nothing.

Alice continued. Faster this time. Stumbling, but determined.

The footsteps were louder. He was coming closer. She held her head high. People can walk the street behind one another, can't they? It's not a crime.

But then, there was the hiding. The skulking in the shadows. His disappearance when she turned to face him. That wasn't right. Her heart thumped in the hollow between her breasts.

This time she would catch him, and she was sure it would be a man, she could tell from the heaviness of his tread. This time she would catch him unawares.

Alice reached into her handbag for a can of underarm spray. She would aim for his eyes. If he was innocent, the spray wouldn't reach. He would be too far behind. If he was creeping up, he would have it right between the eyes.

She held her breath, hand on the can. Waiting. Hoping, he wouldn't be there.

Every hackle raised on her back and neck as she sensed him and bit her lip. Alice was ready.

The steps were maybe two feet behind. She turned and sprayed.

He came at her from the side.

A look of confusion creased her face. She sprayed more, sure that it would put him off, but succeeded only in having the spray blow into her own face. The girl couldn't see him through the chemical-induced tears blurring her vision.

And now, he had hold of her spraying arm, rendering it useless. Her defence gone, she kicked out with a kitten heel, succeeding only in sending her shoe into the road.

Stumbling, she kicked off the other shoe, to keep her balance.

He dragged her off her feet, his sweaty hand over her mouth. She could hear his ragged breathing and struggling only brought on waves of nausea as her head swam.

Alice vomited through his fingers.

He had won. She knew it.

"Come in, Yvonne."

The DI Straightened her skirt, pushing the door open and marvelling at the DCI's ability to see through it. "You wanted to see me, sir?"

"Can you take Dewi and scoot off to Aberystwyth? They found a young woman murdered near the castle, and the MO is the same as a killing several weeks ago. Could be a serial murderer and they have asked for your help."

"Have they?" Yvonne frowned.

Llewellyn shrugged. "You can't blame them. They've heard good things about you."

"I'm surprised they asked for me." Yvonne rubbed the back of her neck. "They have detectives competent enough to investigate this, don't they?"

"I'm sure they have." He nodded. "But, you're not just competent, Yvonne. You are exceptional. Will you take the case or not? I know it will mean commuting-"

"Of course I will." Yvonne held up a hand to stop him

saying anything further. "Give me the location and we'll go there, right away. You don't have to flatter me to get me to do my job."

The DCI tilted his head. "It's not flattery. I will leave a copy of the postmortem report for the previous victim, Kathy Swales, on your desk for when you get back. If you take your iPad, I'll do my best to upload a copy for you to view while you are there."

"Great, thank you."

She ducked out of his office, striding back to her team.

"Dewi?"

"Ma'am?" He turned towards her, breaking off his conversation with Callum.

"We're off to Aberystwyth. They need our help on a case."

"Really?" He raised his eyebrows, hands shifting to his hips.

"Uh huh, serial murder."

Her sergeant cast a wistful glance towards his coffee and shrugged. "I'll go get the car."

THE JOURNEY PASSED by in a blur of countryside, clouds, and Dewi's chatter above the radio.

Yvonne was happy for this. It allowed her to zone in and out, clearing her mind for the horror that was to come.

They approached the castle via the coast road. Walls of water crashed against the sea defences, throwing up vertical fountains and thick flecks of dirty foam. The wind buffeted the car.

Dewi turned the radio off. "We're almost there, ma'am."

They parked next to a grassed area below the castle walls.

Yvonne took a deep breath. "Let's go."

The killer had dumped the body without ceremony. She was naked, her clothes left in a heap.

That the girl had fought for her life was clear in the many defensive bruises littering her limbs and torso.

"He broke her arm." Hanson, the pathologist, stood to greet her. "I'm guessing he did it while trying to subdue her. She died from strangulation, judging from the marks on her neck. Though, as ever, I cannot confirm that until the autopsy."

"I understand." Yvonne nodded. "What's with the tie?" She pointed to the discarded, bloodied material near the girl's left foot.

"I suspect he gagged her with it." Hanson pointed to the girl's mouth. "There's a tiny piece of fabric stuck between her teeth."

"So, why did he remove it from her mouth, only to discard it at the scene?"

Hanson shrugged. "I'll leave the psychology to you guys."

"Thanks." Yvonne clicked her tongue, wondering what Tasha would make of it, scanning her eyes over the grey stone buildings towering over Great Darkgate Street. This was the place where a girl, with her whole future ahead of her, lost her life on the dampest, darkest street corner.

The killer had chosen the spot well. These were not residential buildings, but offices and cafes, probably abandoned at five-thirty to the evening rush hour, and dead in the small hours when he attacked the girl.

No-one to see.

No-one to hear.

The victim was alone, with cold, blind sentinels and the encroaching mist - an enveloping blanket to cover the dead.

One of her socks was missing.

Yvonne snapped a few photographs of her own. Something to help when the two-thirty am work urge overtook her, as it always did when she dealt with murder.

## 2

## SHAUNAGH

The student bar on Aberystwyth University's Penglais campus buzzed, courtesy of a sudden influx after the final lectures of the day.

Shaunagh Keown waited for the girl behind the counter to see her, rueing for the umpteenth time her mousey hair and lack of height. She was invisible. It seemed to her, the tallest and the most striking received preferential treatment.

"Can I help you?"

Shaunagh jumped. "Sorry? Oh, yes. Could I have a large mocha, please?"

The waitress tilted her head. "Cream and caramel with that?"

"Cream but no caramel, thanks." She smiled back at the twinkling eyes of Hannah. That was the name on her badge. Nice name. Nice face.

"Will that be all?"

"Yes, that is everything, thank you." Shaunagh felt for her purse in her bag.

"Two pounds-eighty, please."

She handed over a ten pound note.

"You haven't got anything smaller, have you?"

Shaunagh shook her head.

"No problem." Hannah gave a smile full of straight white teeth.

Shaunagh chose a seat next to a window where she could see people coming and going. Her thoughts turned to the girl killed near the castle.

Alice Brierley had been a student in the biochemistry department. Shaunagh hadn't known her, but felt as though she had. The girl's photograph and life story had been all over the covers of the local newspapers. Her image covered the billboards in the student areas, and the lampposts in the town. Police needed witnesses, those who might have seen Alice as she made her way across town to her student flat in Sea View Place. She couldn't have been more than a few hundred yards from her home when she encountered her killer.

Shaunagh shuddered.

"Have you seen a ghost?" Sparkling eyes were level with hers.

She blinked. "Something like that."

"Mind if I join you? I've just finished a shift. Thought I'd grab a sandwich."

She moved up. "Sure, of course. I'm Shaunagh... Shaunagh Keown."

"Hannah." The girl ripped open her sandwich pack.

"I know."

"You do?"

She nodded towards Hannah's name tag.

"Oh, yeah, of course." Hannah laughed. "You know, I forget I'm wearing it. I thought maybe you had psychic powers. Anyway, my last name is Martin."

"Hannah Martin. It has a ring to it."

"Thanks. At least, you've got some colour back," Hannah said between mouthfuls.

"I was thinking about Alice."

"The girl-"

"Yes." Shaunagh nodded. "The girl who was murdered."

"Did you know her?"

"No. It's shocking, though. It could have been any of us. Poor girl."

Hannah sighed. "Never walk home alone."

"We shouldn't have to live like that, should we? I mean, afraid to be ourselves and walk wherever we like, whatever time we like. Why should women always fear the shadows? Why is this allowed to continue?"

"Because, there is a certain percentage of people who are predators, and the threat of prison is not enough to overcome their urges, I guess." Hannah tilted her head. "You care. I can see. You were putting yourself in Alice's shoes."

"Yes, I suppose I was." Shaunagh wiped coffee froth from her upper lip. "I might have seen him."

"Who?"

"The killer."

"You saw the killer? When?"

She leaned back in her seat. "I was with friends, walking through town along North Parade. I think I might have seen Alice across the road from us. We were heading towards Penglais Hill and she was walking the other way. It was foggy, and I'd had a few drinks, but I'm sure I saw a girl looking like the girl on the posters. There was a man following, about twelve feet behind. Something about him made me uncomfortable."

"What did he look like?"

"I don't know. When I try to recall him, all I see is dark

clothing and mist. That's what I'm remembering. I was tipsy. The memory is vague."

"Have you spoken to police?"

"Not yet, but I've been thinking about it. I don't believe I'd be much use to them, because I can't give a decent description, and I don't know what the time was. I wasn't checking."

Perhaps, your friends might fill in the gaps?" Hannah raised her eyebrows. "I think you ought to talk to the police."

Shaunagh nodded. "I will. I promise."

## 3

## POSTMORTEM

Yvonne had resisted wearing her reading glasses, reluctant to give in to the part of her that was ageing more rapidly than the rest. However, resistance was pointless. Comparing with and without, she had to admit an appreciable difference. She pushed them up her nose before grabbing Kathy Swales postmortem reports.

They made for grim reading.

They had found the first victim of their putative serial killer in the early autumn.

Keith Griffiths, out jogging with his dog, had noticed a woman sitting topless amongst the rocks, looking out to sea.

On closer inspection, he saw her lifeless eyes and cracked skin, pale and mottled. She was dead. Had been for some time.

Bruising to her neck, arms, and torso suggested this was no suicide.

Her killer had left her waist-deep in a rock pool, her clothing discarded to the side.

Griffiths called the police.

According to the statements of her friends, Kathy left

Rummers Wine Bar on Bridge Street after a meal and drinks with them. They were celebrating her nineteenth birthday.

She was a vegan. The friends had chosen Rummers because of its impressive choice of food for vegans. They said she had spent the evening laughing and singing with them, enjoying the food, and looking out over the water.

They had planned to go on to a club, but Kathy cried off, stating she needed to be up early the following day to finish an essay that needed to be in. She insisted they go on to the club without her, her intention being to walk along the seafront, via Pier Street, to her room in Carpenter Hall.

She never made it.

Somewhere between Rummers and Carpenter, she encountered her killer.

Yvonne wondered whether she had gone to the beach voluntarily or whether her killer had coerced her.

The story began with the victims themselves. The important evidence was on their bodies.

HANSON PURSED HIS LIPS. Lines under his eyes were evidence of nights spent working. She understood that, only too well.

"You know, she fought with her attacker for several minutes before he subdued her. Your perp may have injuries he'll be trying to cover up."

Yvonne nodded. "We've carried out a check with local hospitals and GP services and there are no records of anyone presenting themselves for treatment of unexplained injuries. Looks like he hasn't sought help."

"Probably concerned about sticking out, in a small place like this. He'll likely be self-medicating and hiding any injuries from those closest to him." Hanson continued.

"He broke her arm, most likely in the fight but, what seems gratuitous, is that he stuffed the girl's own sock down her throat. I believe he did this after she was already dead."

"Like Kathy Swales. I wondered if that might be the case."

"Yes, she had her underpants pushed down her throat. Again, after she was dead. I can't see any reason for him to do that, other than fulfilling his fantasy."

"The signature." Yvonne shook her head. "His parting shot. I was here."

"Exactly."

"Was she sexually assaulted?"

"He gagged her with a tie, and stripped her, but there was no semen present anywhere inside or outside the body. Also, I don't see any bruising to the inner thighs, that would indicate a rape. There was, however, evidence of recent sexual activity. The presence of spermicide would suggest someone had used a condom. If so, it could have been the perpetrator, but I would say, in that case, he penetrated her after she was already dead."

"A necrophiliac?"

Hanson tilted his head, rubbing his neck. "It's possible. I wouldn't rule it out, though she may have had consensual sex earlier that day, or the previous evening."

"Of course. My officers are out talking to Alice's friends. She didn't have a boyfriend but maybe her friends can point us toward any love interests, casual or otherwise."

Yvonne made to leave, but turned back. "Do you think he removed the gag after she was dead? If that was when he sexually assaulted her, it would fit, wouldn't it?"

"That is perfectly possible. Perhaps he took off the gag, stripped her, and then used a condom."

"Did Kathy Swales have spermicide traces in her? I saw nothing in the report."

"She may have done originally, but he left her in a rock pool. If there were any traces, the water washed them away."

Yvonne nodded. "Thanks, Roger."

"WHAT'S NEW?" Dewi asked, as he popped a cuppa on her desk later that day.

"Postmortem results. Have you seen Kathy Swales' file?"

Dewi shook his head.

"Well, you need to. I'm wondering if the killer is from that part of town. Perhaps, he lives near the harbour or the castle area and lies in wait for potential victims."

"It two months between murders, wasn't it?"

"Six weeks. That's not a particularly long cooling-off period. It means we have to move on this."

"Right." Dewi nodded.

"I'll leave the file with you." Yvonne took a sip from her mug. "In the meantime, I would like you to go through the sex offender register, looking for all those living within the Aberystwyth area. Make a note of any who have a predilection for necrophilia or necrophilia-related pornography."

Dewi pulled a face, his disgust clear.

"You think he's a necrophiliac?"

She shrugged. "On the evidence we have so far, that it is a distinct and unpleasant possibility."

"Nasty."

"Yes. He stuffed Kathy's underpants down her throat. He did this after she was already dead. He did the same with Alice Brierley. Only, in her case, used a sock. It wasn't necessary to silence them. It was an additional thing, after he strangled them. He did it for his own gratification, perhaps, while he was sexually assaulting them, wearing a condom."

"I can't imagine being that sick."

"Let me know if you find anything relevant in the records of the offenders you dig up."

"Will do."

Yvonne watched Dewi disappear down the corridor, deep in thought, then gathered her briefing notes in readiness for the two Aberystwyth DCs assigned to work with her. She was looking forward to meeting Sarah Evans and Ifan Hughes.

## 4

## NIGHT PORTER

"You're late." Mark Bennett's colleague, Fran Owen, looked him up and down, tutting and shaking her head.

He straightened his blue polo shirt, hastily donned not five minutes before. "Sorry...," he said, looking at his feet, smoothing his hair as the heat rose in his cheeks. "Thanks for covering for me." He glanced left and right along the corridor.

"Fine, but I can't keep covering. If Heston finds out you went walkies again, you'll be for it and so will I." She was referring to Paul Heston, otherwise known as The Fuhrer, the man in charge of Bronglais Hospital's porter staff, known for his quick temper and sharp tongue.

"I know."

"Where were you, anyway?"

He bit his lower lip. "My mum is poorly. I went to check on her. You know how it is."

"Do I?" She balled her fists, placing them on her ample hips.

"I won't do it again."

"You said that last time." Fran grabbed one end of the trolley. "We've got to move a patient from A&E to Meurig ward."

"No problem."

"Are you sure you're ready?"

"Yeah."

As they manoeuvred the trolley along the corridor, Mark's skin prickled. Eyes were everywhere, scrutinising him. Judging him.

He knew it.

Sweat poured down his temples and from his forehead, onto his cheeks and into his eyebrows. He wiped it away with the top of his forearm.

The heavily sedated patient was out. Mark was pleased about that, as it meant he didn't need to make small-talk. It gave him time to think. As soon as they deposited their charge on Meurig, Mark headed for his locker, telling Fran he was fetching his sandwiches.

He checked both ways, heart smashing inside his chest walls, turning the key in his locker.

Mopping more sweat, he reached his hand in. The dress and other items were still there. He hadn't really thought anyone would take them, but his uneasiness was growing. He should store them elsewhere. And soon.

## 5

## TEAMWORK

DC Sarah Evans towered over her male colleague DC Ifan Hughes.

Yvonne did a double-take, stifling the surprise on her face and hoping they hadn't noticed. There had to be at least a foot difference between the two. She chided herself for thinking in stereotype, something she didn't appreciate in others.

"Yvonne Giles." She held out her hand.

Sarah shook it first, followed by Ifan, concentration clear in the lines on their expectant faces.

"I'm waiting for DS Dewi Hughes to join us and we can get started." She forwarded the projector to photographs of the dead girls.

Sarah turned her blue eyes to the door. "I think that might be him." She gestured towards Dewi, who stopped in the doorway to catch his breath.

"Ah, Dewi. Good of you to join us." Yvonne grinned.

"Sorry," Dewi grimaced. "I lost track of time. I've been going through sex offender records."

"You got anything?"

"I've got several names." Dewi shrugged. "But there is no necrophilic history."

"That's okay." The DI ran a hand through her hair. "We'll work with what we've got. Even if he is a necrophiliac, there's no guarantee they'll have caught him for it before. There's a first time for everything."

"Necrophilia? Really?" Ifan shuddered. "Yuck."

Yvonne tapped her laser pen on her chin. "As you'll see, it's a possibility. But, I stress, it is only a possibility based on the limited information we have."

She outlined the details of the cases for each of the girls, finishing with, "It's possible that this predator prowls that part of town, waiting for potential victims, seeking lone females under the influence. I do not think this is an outsider coming in. He is too aware of his surroundings and confident of not being caught in the act."

"You don't think maybe he stalks them first then?" Ifan asked, his brow furrowed. He flicked his sandy fringe out of his eyes.

"Well, obviously we can't rule that out. What we have, however, is two victims killed at the top of town. So, we start there. This will be an area very familiar to him. He may live or work there."

"Right." Ifan scribbled into his pad.

Yvonne noted his chewed fingernails, wondering if he suffered with anxiety.

"Should we request extra uniformed patrols for the castle area?" Sarah asked, putting her pen down.

Yvonne nodded. "For the time being, we have extra uniformed officers in place, and they are doing what they can to reassure the public. But what we say in our briefings stays in our briefings. The only communication with outside must be through official news conferences. Is that okay with everyone?"

Each murmured their agreement.

"Great, let's talk to witnesses. I will speak to the guy who found Kathy Swales' body. He may have seen someone hanging around. The killer left her sitting up, looking out to sea. Maybe, he wanted to watch her discovery and observe the finder's reaction to the crime."

"Wouldn't be the first time we've seen that." Dewi nodded. "Right, better get to it."

Yvonne paused. "Also, Ifan and Sarah, would you mind going around all the shops and restaurants on Bridge Street, Pier Street, Great Darkgate Street, and North Parade. Get a hold of any CCTV they have for the nights when Kathy and Alice died. They may have caught the girls walking past and, more importantly, they may have caught their killer. Check with uniform before you do, as it is likely they are already examining footage. If not, we may have lost the opportunity to have any for Kathy. Get on it fast as you can."

"Yes, ma'am." Ifan nodded, chivalrously holding the door open for her and Sarah.

KEITH GRIFFITHS, a forty-five-year-old lecturer of Law at the university, put on his reading glasses to examine the photograph handed to him by Yvonne. He pushed them atop his receding hairline as he reverted his attention back to her. "Yes, that is the young woman I discovered in the rock pools."

Yvonne flicked her eyes over his smart-casual attire of black jeans, white shirt, grey jumper, and a university scarf hanging loose around his neck. The muscles in his face didn't move, making it hard to read his thoughts. It didn't seem right for him to appear relaxed after he had discovered a dead girl and was being interviewed in a police station. But he did.

She cleared her throat. "You were out walking your dog?"

"Yes." He nodded. "We go the same route every morning. It's convenient, as we live the other side of the harbour. I take Benji, that's my Jack Russell terrier, over the bridge and through to the pier, walking around the castle. Benji always gets to the beach before I do. Well, that day as usual, he was first down there and I could hear him barking non-stop. He shot off, and I thought that strange. When I got to him, he was barking at what I thought was a girl bathing in a rock pool, in the freezing cold. It surprised me, but people do strange things, don't they?"

"When did you realise the girl was dead?"

"I didn't realise she was deceased until I was a few feet away. I thought it strange, I hadn't seen her move. Then I noticed her colouring, and I felt my stomach knotting. I was sure before I touched her that she was dead."

"You touched her?"

"Yes, on the arm. She was stiff. Her eyes were... were... She was staring out to sea. I'm sorry, can I have a minute?" He took out a handkerchief and blew his nose. "I called the police straight away."

"Mr Griffiths, did you see anyone else? When you found the girl, I mean. Was anyone leaving the area or hanging around?"

He looked to his left as though recalling the scene. He shook his head. "Nobody else was on the beach, that I remember. I looked both ways along the sand for help and didn't see another soul. I can't explain it, but I felt exposed."

"It was a frightening situation."

"Well, I mean, I had seen others around on the promenade. They were walking along the pavement up top. It was around six in the morning. But the beach was empty, save for the dead girl."

"Had you ever seen the girl before?"

"Who me?" He paused. "Not really."

"That's a little vague-"

"I may have seen her in passing, but I didn't know her." He shifted in his seat, adjusting his scarf.

"What was your impression when you found her?"

He shrugged. "I thought maybe she had taken something intending to kill herself or, perhaps, she had been at a beach party the night before and taken drugs. She could have overdosed, causing those with her to panic and run. However, when I saw the bruises around her neck, I realised someone had murdered her. After realising that, I wondered whether the killer had staged her to shock us. And I wondered if he was watching me."

Yvonne nodded. "We wondered that, too."

"Sorry I couldn't be more help with that. My glances up and down the beach were brief. He could have been there, and I just didn't spot him."

Yvonne smiled. "It's okay. You've been very helpful. We may need to talk to you again."

He nodded, rising from his chair. "You can reach me at the University."

## 6

## FOLLOWER IN THE DARK

Hannah yawned as she finished washing the glasses behind the student bar. She needed her bed and sleep. It had been a long day. Too long.

The icy temperature raised the hairs on her arms as she wheeled her bike out of the covered racks. It turned her breath to vapour clouds that blurred the outline of the Stanley Knife ahead of her, the bell tower, so named because it looked like the workman's tool.

Another freezing fog was moving in from the sea. Hannah mounted and pushed off. A squelching, and her bike's resistance to movement meant one thing. Puncture.

"Damn it." She jumped down to look. The front tyre was flat. It should have been a pedal-free joy ride into town, but would now be a swift walk in the freezing cold. She sighed, checking her watch. Eleven-fifteen. Not a good time to be walking alone. The night bus would be another fifteen minutes. She could be home in that time if she got a move on. Besides, manoeuvring her bicycle in and out of the bus was not something she relished.

Walk it was.

John Loyd, a university security guard, saw her from his box at the entrance of Penglais campus, at the turnoff from the Hill of the same name.

He watched her, as she wheeled her bike looking cheesed off, and looked at the clock. "I'll be knocking off in five minutes, Mal," he called to the colleague who had just joined him for the handover.

"Go now, if you want to," Mal offered, donning his uniform jacket and blowing on his hands.

"You sure?"

"Yeah, 'course."

"Thanks, mate." Lloyd grabbed his bag, stuffing his cap into it. "Have a good one."

Mal pulled a face. "I'll try."

Lloyd's six-foot-two frame cast a long shadow in the light from the box as he crossed the driveway towards the hill and his walk down into town.

HANNAH WAS glad of the wide pavement along Penglais Hill. The traffic was noisy and regular. It made her uncomfortable. Perhaps it was the discovery of the dead girls, but she felt it might be all too easy for the occupants of some passing vehicle to abduct a person.

She walked as far away from the curb as possible.

In the distance, she could see the mist covering the town whose lights had faded because of it. Her thoughts turned to Alice Brierley on the night she met her death. That same mist. A shiver travelled up and down her spine.

"You walking?"

She jumped, spinning round, heart thudding in her

chest. She didn't speak, but stared wide-eyed at her unwanted companion.

"I just mean you are walking your bike instead of riding it." John Lloyd's shadow stretched far ahead as he caught up to her.

"I have a puncture." The words came from between clenched teeth.

"I didn't scare you did I?" He tilted his head to better see her face.

*Keep walking. Why don't you just keep walking?* Hannah pushed her bicycle forward. "I'm fine, just in a hurry to get home. There are people waiting for me."

"I'll walk you down."

*No.* "I'm fine, honestly. It won't take me long." She recognised him. Knew he was the new security guard at the campus. She didn't like the way he stared or the way his eyebrows met in the middle. It made him appear predatory. Or, perhaps, it was those traits, mixed with his enormous height and muscular bulk. She felt vulnerable.

"Still, you don't know who's about and I'm going your way, anyway-" The words were slow and soft. It didn't help.

"I don't need an escort." She cut him dead, anger in her voice. Fight or flight. She had chosen. Fight.

"Fine. No need to be like that." He moved in front, hurrying towards town. He didn't look back.

Hannah sighed, the tension in her body easing with a sigh. *Thank God for that.*

THE FOLLOWING MORNING, a pained look on her sergeant's face stopped Yvonne in her tracks. "Dewi? What is it?"

"Ma'am, dump your files. We've got another murder to attend." He shook his head. "He struck again."

The DI swallowed hard. "Who? Where?"

"Another young female. We don't have an identity, yet. They found her body near the kicking bar at the foot of Constitution Hill."

She knew Dewi referred to the metal railings below the cliff top at one end of Aberystwyth bay, just along from the former court and police station. She had visited them several times with Tasha, kicking them and making a wish as was the custom.

"Oh, dear God, no." She ran a hand through her hair. "Grab your coat. Let's go."

Thick cumulus clouds filled the sky, drizzling on a town rendered grey by their shadows.

Yvonne pulled her mac tightly around her, a sinking feeling gnawing her innards. This was what she dreaded. Not even six week's grace this time. The murderer was upping his game.

Uniformed officers worked hard to keep onlookers behind the cordons. They had erected a tent over the body, but SOCO had only just begun their work.

Yvonne and Dewi suited up, donning masks before flashing their ID's and going inside.

The victim was petite, dark-haired, and naked. Her clothing, similar to previous victims', discarded in a heap near her feet. She had multiple bruises on her torso, arms, and throat, and her right temple had a two-inch gash, as though he had hit her with something blunt and heavy. Her dark hair lay in thick tangles.

"He beats them, Dewi. Why does he do that? It's over the top. If he intends killing them anyway, why not hit them hard and incapacitate them? Why the beatings? What does that do for him?"

"I thought we agreed they were putting up a fight for their lives?" Dewi frowned.

"Yes, but why? I mean, why is he giving them the opportunity to fight back? It suggests a high level of confidence in his ability to bring them under control, doesn't it? Anything could go wrong, surely?" Yvonne pursed her lips, thinking. "No, Dewi, he gets something from it. He wants them to fight back. It's all part of it for him."

"Maybe it gives him an excuse to kill them. Perhaps he can't bring himself to kill unless they fight back. Make him angry." Dewi shook his head as though doubting his own words.

"That's a good point. You may have something there, Dewi." Yvonne crouched to examine the girl's clothing with gloved hands. She looked towards the SOCO officer at the tent's entrance. "Has the photographer been?"

"Yes," the female SOCO confirmed.

"Thanks." The DI sifted through the items. "Her bra is missing, Dewi. I'd put money on them finding it in her oesophagus."

Dewi grimaced.

Yvonne stood, gesturing to the female SOCO. "When the pathologist gets here, ask him to make sure they check her intimate areas for spermicide. I know he would likely check, anyway, but I want to make sure."

"Of course." The female SOCO wiped drizzle from her glasses with her sleeve. "The body is still warm."

"Is it?" Yvonne placed a gloved hand on the dead girl's arm.

"Not so much her extremities, but her midriff area."

Yvonne felt the warmth. Not normal body temperature but warm. "Suggests he attacked her this morning?"

"That is probable. Likely, just before it got light."

Yvonne looked over the jogging bottoms and top. "She was probably out for an early morning run along the seafront. Poor kid." She sighed, rising to her feet.

As they left the tent, the DI glanced around at the buildings nearby.

"Halls of residence." Dewi confirmed.

"Make sure uniform to talk to all who were in those buildings this morning. There are a lot of windows. Someone must have seen something."

"Will do."

"I wonder if he's baiting us, Dewi, leaving her so close to the old station."

Dewi nodded. "Maybe."

"When can we have an ID?"

"Sarah and Ifan are on it, ma'am. Someone will report her missing, if they haven't already."

Yvonne pursed her lips. "The news will devastate her family."

"There was a piece in the paper yesterday, it suggested the killer's haunt was the top of town."

"Really? Perhaps this is his answer. They say the top, so he leaves one at the bottom."

"Would be awful to think this girl died because the killer wanted to prove a point." Dewi frowned.

"I know, and it's happened before. The sort of killer that loves the limelight, and his photo in the papers, gets annoyed if they don't get the details right. I'll wager he's scouring all the papers he can lay his hands on. I think we need to give our newspaper friends some timely reminders. They must act responsibly."

7

## SOMBRE DAY

When the Ifan handed her the dead girl's details, Yvonne was in the middle of drafting timelines with the salient points for each murder. She had placed a map in the centre of the board and plotted where they had found the bodies, adding photographs of the girls and their murder scenes, and writing out the basic details for each of the victims next to their names.

Her train of thought interrupted, she turned to the young DC. "Sorry, yes?"

"Ma'am, I think the girl found this morning is eighteen-year-old Amanda Hartnett, a first-year student studying art at the university."

"Eighteen? Oh my goodness, she was barely out of childhood," Yvonne murmured, her eyes, soulful.

"She was originally from Solihull in Birmingham. Some of her college friends are heading over to the morgue to identify her."

"Have they informed her family?" Yvonne ran a hand through her hair, wondering if the task would fall to her.

"I think the crime commissioner is handling it, personally," Ifan said, as though he had read her thoughts.

"Is he?"

"Yes," Ifan confirmed. "And I've heard the university have agreed to put the families of the dead girls in accommodation in Aberystwyth, whilst they come to terms with what has happened to their loved ones."

Yvonne nodded. "That is something at least. I don't envy them the pain they are going through."

"I can see you've been busy, ma'am." Ifan cast his eyes over Yvonne's handiwork.

"Yes, I've been plotting out the main details. I can use it for the briefing tomorrow and try to get my head around it all today."

"Do you think there's a method to all this?" Ifan frowned as he examined her work.

"I don't know. I was hoping to spot a pattern. I haven't, yet. He may pick girls and locations at random but, if he doesn't, the sooner we get what he's up to, the better."

"Agreed."

Yvonne added the newly printed photograph of Amanda Hartnett to her board. "Victim number three. Pray God we have no more, Ifan."

Shaunagh Keown waited in reception in the police station on the Boulevard De Saint Brieuc in Aberystwyth. She possessed a petite frame and a shock of curly red hair. It was almost too much hair for one so small. She frequently pushed it off her face.

"Shaunagh?" Yvonne held the door open.

"Yes, that's me." The girl rose to her feet and made her way over to the DI.

"Thank you for coming in at such short notice." She motioned the girl to a chair in the interview room. "You must forgive me if I flounder, this is not my usual station."

Shaunagh shrugged. "No problem."

Yvonne smiled. "I understand you saw Alice Brierley's killer?"

The girl cringed, her cheeks colouring. "Possibly, I can't be sure. I rang you because I thought I saw Alice on the night she was murdered. She was being followed by a male in dark clothing. He could have been her killer but, equally, he could be innocent."

"Aha." Yvonne threw back her head. "The message must have gotten exaggerated on its way to me. Can you walk me through where you were and what happened?"

"Of course. I'd been out for a meal and drinks with my friends. We were making our way through town intending to walk up Penglais Hill to our halls of residence."

"Where were you when you saw Alice?"

"The girl I saw was walking in the opposite direction to us. We were heading along North Parade and she was on the other side of the road. I remember it was foggy but, when I saw the photograph of the dead girl... well, I was fairly sure it was her I had seen that night. The hairstyle and jacket were the same as those on the posters."

"What about the person you saw behind her?"

"Well, it was dark and foggy, like I said, but he appeared taller than Alice. I would say at least a foot taller. I would have put him at around six feet or more in height. He hunched himself over, his head down, like he was trying to be invisible. I thought he looked suspicious. He was wearing a black or dark cap and dark clothing. He had his hands stuffed into the pockets of his jacket."

"And his build?"

"I can't be sure, but I think he was average build, with an oversized jacket."

"Did anything else make you feel suspicious of his intentions?"

Shaunagh shrugged. "It was the feeling I had about him. He was furtive, like he wanted us to ignore him. I don't know, maybe I was reading too much into it. He made me feel uncomfortable for the girl. If it had been me he was following, I would have felt scared."

"Did you say anything to your friends?"

"I tapped my friend Brian on the shoulder and said the guy gave me the creeps. By then, however, the girl and man had disappeared up the street and we couldn't see them anymore. Brian suggested they might have been a couple who had had a quarrel, and the boyfriend was just catching up to her. That wasn't my impression. I was tipsy, though, so I could have misread the situation and the guy may have been innocent."

"It concerned you enough to contact us." The DI tilted her head, her voice soft.

"Yes, I was sure he was up to something. I contacted you because what I saw could have been relevant and I wouldn't forgive myself if I left you unaware of some important detail that could make a difference."

"Well, we are very glad you came forward. We couldn't do our jobs without the help of the public. Information from people like yourself is crucial. Sometimes, it is the seemingly insignificant details that crack the case."

Shaunagh smiled, colouring again. "That makes me feel better."

"Do you know what the time was, Shaunagh?"

She shook her head. "No. I think it would have been around half-past one but, in all honesty, it could have been twenty minutes either side of that. I know I was in bed by half-past two."

"Would your friends know more accurately?"

"I can ask them and let you know."

"That would be good. Is there anything else you'd like to tell me?"

Shaunagh shook her head. "No, no, I think that is everything."

"Well, thank you for your time." Yvonne stood. "I'll see you out."

8

## EVERYONE'S A SUSPECT

Hannah returned to the waiting room of Ceredigion Dental Practice holding the side of her face.

"Are you okay?" Shaunagh frowned. "They hurt you?"

"Filling," Hannah mumbled, wiping a dribble from the corner of her mouth. "I hate needles."

"You and me both." Shaunagh gave her back the bag she had been holding. "I thought you said you weren't expecting treatment today? Don't worry." She held her hand up. "Don't answer that. We can talk later, when the anaesthetic has worn off."

They set off back to the campus on foot, appreciating the clearest skies they had had in a while. The temperature had dropped once more, leaving the air crisp. Frost covered the grass and the hedges.

"I don't like him." Hannah announced as they neared the top of Penglais Hill, intending to have lunch at the Arts Centre before their afternoon lectures.

"Who?"

"Creighton the dentist."

"Oh, right, nobody likes dentists when they are in the chair."

"He gives me the creeps." Hannah wiped her lip. "He hovers. I swear I caught him trying to look down my top."

"Really?" Shaunagh frowned. "Can't say that I have noticed him doing that to me, but I haven't been for a while. I can't remember what he was like."

Hannah tutted. "Shame he's one of the few NHS dentists left. I can't afford to go private."

"None of us can." Shaunagh put a hand on Hannah's shoulder. "I'm sure he meant no harm. Some people can't help themselves. I don't think they realise they are doing it?"

"Really?" Hannah raised her eyebrow.

"Well, probably not. I'm just trying to cheer you up. Come on now, girl, how is that gum? Ready for some soup?"

∽

MARK BENNETT LICKED the sweat from his upper lip, checking both ways along the corridor before grabbing the items of clothing from his locker and stuffing them into a holdall. He had his back to the CCTV camera, just in case the security guard was looking at it.

His shirt stuck to his back. He didn't like carrying things around with him. People were incapable of minding their own business. He hated having to do things he didn't want to.

"You clocking off?"

He jumped, the holdall slipping from his grip before he had secured the zip.

It was Fran.

He stuffed the clothing back in, not daring to look her in the face. His breath came in ragged bursts.

"Those for your mum?"

"Yeah," he grunted.

"Is she any better?"

"She's getting there." He remained with his back to her.

"Oh." Fran frowned. "Well, I hope she continues to be on the mend."

"Thanks. I've got to run. I've got a mountain of stuff to do." He turned to leave.

"I'll be leaving soon, too." Fran held up a Sterlin vial. "I said I'd run this sample over to the lab."

"Right." Bennett breathed deep, shouldering the holdall. "I'll be off. See you tomorrow?" Finally, he looked at her.

"Yes, see you tomorrow. I'll be in early."

"Right." He set off down the corridor, not looking back. He knew she would watch him walk away, a puzzled look on her face. She liked him. Really liked him. And that made him uncomfortable. He couldn't want her back. His tastes were not that simple."

∼

CHLOE GARSFORTH WAS in her second year, studying law.

Hannah had only known her for six months but the two had become good friends in that time, though their subjects could hardly have been more different, the latter studying agriculture. She met her outside, and they walked up the steps towards the Arts Centre.

"I am so glad to get out of there." Chloe huffed, her shoulder-length blonde hair falling loose from her ponytail; her day-old mascara knotting her eyelashes.

"Why? What happened?" Hannah grabbed Chloe's books while the latter put on her jacket.

"Adam bloody Hardy. Oh my God, he does my head in." She sighed. "You know what he did today?"

Hannah giggled. "No, what did he do?"

"He came into lectures twenty minutes late. Then, barely having sat down, he shouts out to the lecturer, 'Can you repeat that, please?' When the tutor asked him which bit, he shouted, 'The last twenty minutes.' Unbelievable."

Hannah laughed from her belly. "Oh, I wish I'd been there to see your lecturer's face."

"It's not funny. He disrupted the whole session. He's such an attention-seeker. He comes in, spreading his arms, as if to say, 'look at me'. The guy is an asshole."

"There's at least one on every course, and not always male." Hannah laughed. "Don't think about it, if it upsets you. For all you know, he may have autism or something similar. Maybe he can't help the way he is. How would you feel if that were to be the case? Hmm?"

Chloe grimaced. "I'd feel bad for judging him."

"Exactly. Whenever I find someone or something annoying, I think of potential reasons behind it and I stop feeling upset. Better for me and better for everyone else."

Chloe grinned. "I love how you are always so cool and collected. That is why we are friends."

"Obviously." Hannah gave Chloe back her books. "Let's grab that coffee. I am working in the bar, later."

Chloe paused. "You know he has followed girls home before now?"

"Really?" Hannah turned to her, her forehead furrowed. "When?"

"He does it all the time. Begs people to go out with him

or to let him into their rooms for a coffee. He asked me to go back to his room, once."

"Well, if people are avoiding him, he probably gets lonely." Hannah said this to reassure her friend but felt uneasy as they continued their walk up the steps to the bar. The spate of murders in the town had everyone jumpy.

## 9

## PROGRESS?

DC Sarah Evans had her head down, scribbling furiously onto a notepad and chewing on her pen whenever she paused.

"Everything okay, Sarah?" Yvonne approached her desk, impressed by the young DC's studiousness.

"I was just about to find you, ma'am." Sarah looked up, her eyes sparkling. "I've just taken a call from one Francis Owen, who states she is a porter at Bronglais Hospital."

"Okay..."

"She said she was responding to our appeals for information in connection with the deaths of the female students."

Yvonne perched on Sarah's desk. "Hit me."

"She said one of her male colleagues, Mark Bennett, has been acting suspiciously. He's been disappearing during shift hours and she has been covering for him. They often do the late or very early shifts." Sarah checked her notes. "He was absent for over an hour, from five-fifteen, on the morning of Amanda Hartnett's murder. She said he came back sweating and looking sheepish, thanking her for covering for him again."

"Did he really? Interesting. Nice work. I think we'll get him in and have a little chat."

"There's something else. She said he dropped his bag in the corridor when she surprised him a week ago. She said several items of women's clothing fell out of his bag, including underwear. She reckons he'd been hiding them in his lockers. He jumped a mile when she came up behind him as he was transferring them from the locker to the bag."

"Really? Then we should definitely get him in. Could yourself and Ifan go see Francis Owen in person? Be discreet, I don't want her colleague to know she has spoken to us until we can guarantee her safety. Get a statement from her and more details regarding dates and times of absences and any other information she might have regarding his routines, etcetera. In the meantime, I will take Dewi and see if we can catch up with Mark Bennett away from the hospital. Could you telephone Bronglais Hospital and ask for a contact number, mobile if possible, for Bennett?"

"I could, ma'am."

"Thanks, Sarah. Good work."

∾

DEWI CAME INTO THE OFFICE, striding over to the DI.

"Aha, Dewi, could you run a check for me? On a Mark Bennett, a forty-year-old porter at Bronglais Hospital? His date of Birth is the thirteenth of January, nineteen-eighty. His address is on this." She handed him an information sheet. "I want a full PNC check and details of any convictions, if you have the time?"

"Mark Bennett?" Dewi frowned. "That name rings a bell.

I think it was one name on my sex offenders list. I'll check it out, anyway. Do you want it now?"

"Yes, Dewi, now." She grinned, adding, "Please."

"No problem." He waved a hand at her before going back the way he had come.

∼

"WHAT HAVE YOU GOT FOR ME?" Yvonne asked, as Dewi returned.

"As I thought, he was on my list of people to check. Two previous convictions for stealing women's clothing, particularly underwear, from washing lines."

"Really?"

"He completed two probation orders, one twelve years ago, and the other, seven years ago. They were for two hundred hours of community work, and two hundred hours with eighteen months supervision, respectively. He hasn't come to our attention since then but, it would appear, he may have continued offending."

Yvonne pursed her lips. "Where is my partner when I need her? I'm sure Tasha would confirm that a paraphilia, such as his, is often present in the background of serious sexual offenders and serial killers. Is he escalating?"

"Shall we pick him up?"

"No. Let's invite him in. All we have at the moment are old convictions and the suspicions of a colleague. I don't want to draw attention to this guy if he is innocent and has worked hard at rebuilding his life. We'll interview him here and see what he has to say about his absences."

∼

MARK BENNETT LOOKED to be about six feet in height and strong. Strong enough to subdue a slight young woman with relative ease, Yvonne thought, as she seated herself opposite him in the interview room.

He had slicked his dark hair back with gel. Sweat dribbled down his temples. He flicked her a quick look before his eyes reverted to the papers in front of her.

She had expected their killer to be confident. The man in front of her appeared anything but. "Do you know why you are here, Mark?" She asked in a soft voice.

He looked up. "No." His eyes dropped back to the table.

"Are you aware that someone murdered three young women in Aberystwyth in the last couple of months?"

"Of course I am, who wouldn't be? You'd have to be blind and deaf. It's all I've seen on the news and in the papers." His brow furrowed. "Wait a minute, you don't think I-"

"We are talking to everyone with previous sexual convictions," Yvonne interjected, aware that if he remained taut as he was, she would get little from him."

"I did courses for the mistakes I made. Not that I needed them." He ran his tongue over his upper lip.

"What do you mean, you didn't need them?" Yvonne leaned in, tilting her head. "You stole women's clothing."

"I'm not a sex offender."

"Stealing underwear from washing lines is-"

"It's not what you think." She felt spray from his mouth as he spat the words. He glared at her.

*So he has a temper.* She leaned back in her chair, running a handkerchief over her chin. "So, enlighten me. What was it, if not what I think?"

"I don't have to go through it with you. I didn't steal knickers because I got off on them."

"What then?"

*Death in the Mist* 43

"I needed them."

"What?"

"I wanted some, and I thought it wouldn't hurt to snag a pair, or two, from washing lines."

"Why didn't you just go down the shops like everyone else?"

"I didn't want to."

"Where were you Tuesday, around six in the morning?"

"Well, that's easy. I was working. Go look at the rota, you'll see. I work at the hospital. I'm a porter."

"I know." Yvonne sighed. "I also know that you were not there, when you should have been."

He had a pained look as though holding his breath and dreading what was coming next.

"So, I ask again, where were you?"

"This is Fran, isn't it?" he blurted. She has a thing for me. She can't have me, so she's making up stories."

"We've checked hospital CCTV. It shows you leaving just before five-fifteen. Where did you go?"

He began chewing his thumbnail. "I had a call from the care home. I went to see my mother. She has dementia." He slumped in his chair, placing his elbows on the table and putting his head in his hands. "Pant Glas. Look them up. My mum is Harriet Bennett. They will confirm what I told you."

"Why didn't you inform the hospital of where you were going?"

"Fran knew. She always knows. I always tell her."

The CCTV shows you stuffing items from your locker in a holdall. It looks like female clothing."

"It was mine. Gym stuff. No female clothing, I'm afraid."

"Are you sure?"

"Yes. Can I go now?"

"Mark, did you go anywhere near Constitution Hill at six am on Tuesday morning?"

"What? Why... Oh, you think I killed that girl. The one they found on the front, near Bath Steps. You think I did it, don't you?"

"We're making inquiries. I'm not accusing you of anything. You were absent from your place of work at the time someone murdered her and you chose not to inform your employers. I believe that gives me the right to ask the question. I am a police officer. It's what I do." Yvonne leaned in once more. "You've told me that you were at the care home. I can look into that, of course. I still want a direct answer to my question."

"Then, no, I did not go anywhere near Constitution Hill on Tuesday. Now, can I go?"

"Yes, There's no reason to keep you. You are free to leave."

"Thanks."

He scraped his chair back and rose to go.

"I may wish to talk to you again, Mark. And, just to remind you, we got our information from CCTV, we didn't need to hear it from any of your colleagues."

∽

"How did it go?" Dewi asked her as she returned to the main office.

"Difficult." She rubbed her forehead. "He's hiding something. It could be something as harmless as cross-dressing, or it could be murder. We need to contact the care home his mother is in and check if he was there on Tuesday morning. He claims she has dementia, and they regularly call him in to help with her."

"What about the women's clothing he had in his locker?"

"Denies it completely. Said it was his gym clothes."

"He's probably stealing it again, isn't he?"

"That's a strong possibility." Yvonne nodded. "He's a complex character and one we definitely need to monitor. In the meantime, I will pop over to the care home and do some digging."

10

## GAPS

Susan Lewis had been Alice Brierley's closest friend since the latter arrived at the university as a fresher.

Twenty-one-year-old Susan claimed to know everything there was to know about Alice because they shared the top-floor flat at Moravon in Sea View Place. Both were studying biochemistry.

Wearing jeans and a Wales rugby shirt, Susan sported carefully applied makeup and perfectly manicured nails, that seemed at odds with the casual look. Her demure demeanour and large eyes tempted one to believe everything that came out of her mouth. Perversely, that made Yvonne want to question everything. It was clear from the lines under her eyes, however, Susan had done her fair share of crying and lying awake.

"So, you stated that Alice hadn't been intimate with anyone in the forty-eight hours prior to her death?" The DI settled back on the mud-brown sofa in the tiny lounge. The mismatched, second hand furniture screamed student rental.

"That's right. I was out with her on the night they killed

her. She wasn't into toilet sex and, even if she was, she was never away long enough to have indulged in any. She didn't have a boyfriend and hadn't been in a relationship with one for months, since she split with her boyfriend back home. I am as certain as I can be that she was not intimate with anyone in the days before her death."

"And back home was London, right?"

"Enfield, yes."

"Had she heard from her ex-boyfriend?"

"Not that I am aware. She said they had agreed the split because of the distance involved. Her ex was moving to Spain to work in a bar."

"Do you know his name?"

"No, I didn't ask her."

"And she didn't see him around here?"

"No, I am sure she would have mentioned something if she had."

"She texted you, didn't she? As she was walking home?"

"She did. It wasn't long after she left us waiting for the night bus."

"What did the text say?"

"See you back at the flat."

"That's it? Nothing else?"

"Nothing else. It's easy to misread texts, I know, but I took that to be an apology for not waiting with us. A kind of way for her to say, 'I'm not in a huff or anything. I'm fine.' I think maybe she thought we would worry that we had done something wrong, or that I might worry that I had offended her."

"I see."

"When you found her, was her phone with her?"

Yvonne nodded. "Yes."

"Then, why did you need to ask me what text she sent?"

"someone had wiped the message history from the phone."

"The killer?"

"We don't know. If it was the killer, he wore gloves. The only prints we found were Alice's, but why would Alice want to delete her message history? We should know, eventually, what texts were on the phone. Our tech guys are the best. But in the meantime, I thought I would ask."

Susan scoured the DI's face, but said nothing further.

Yvonne stood to leave. "I know our SOCO guys took some of her things away. They will return them to you and to her family when they have finished with them. I hope it hasn't caused you too much disruption."

"Compared to the loss of Alice, it was no disruption."

Yvonne nodded. "I would think it wasn't. Well, I will let you get on. Please contact me if you have any concerns or if you have further information, you think relevant."

"I will," Susan said as she showed the DI to the door.

∽

PANT GLAS CARE Home stood on the coast above Aberystwyth and, from one side, had fine views of the sea.

Yvonne could see and hear the gulls circling above and hoped they wouldn't poop on her.

A blonde-haired, sporty-looking woman in her thirties, wearing a pink carer's uniform, came to the main entrance of the sizeable Victorian sprawl. "Pam Williams." She held out a hand. "You must be Inspector Giles."

"Yes, Yvonne Giles," the DI shook the offered hand. "Thank you for seeing me at short notice."

"Come in. I'll take you to our office. I'm the general manager." Pam walked to a counter and scribbled in a book.

She had a gentle voice. Yvonne could imagine her being very good with the elderly residents.

When they reached the office, Pam showed her to an easy chair. "How can I help?" she asked, seating herself.

"I'm here to ask you about Harriet Bennett and her son, Mark Bennett."

"Ah, yes. Harriet. She is one of our younger residents at sixty-seven."

"I understand she suffers from dementia?"

"That's right. It's gotten progressively worse. She's been here for eighteen months, now. Mark provides additional support, when he is able."

"I see. That is what I wanted to ask you about, actually. Can you tell me if he was here at six in the morning, last Tuesday?"

Pam shook her head. "I don't think so."

"You don't think? Does that mean you don't know?"

"I don't remember his being here but we can check with the register, and we will know for sure. Everyone who comes here has to ring the bell and we log them in and log them out."

"I came in without being logged in." Yvonne frowned.

"That's because I signed you in the diary, myself."

"I see, so that is what you were doing at the counter?" Yvonne's smile stretched across her face. "Can we check it, now?"

"Sure. We'll go back to reception."

The register was open on the countertop. Pam flicked to the relevant date, turning it towards the detective. "There you go, he definitely wasn't here last Tuesday."

"Are you sure that he couldn't have come in unbeknown to anyone?"

"Sure. As I say, all who come here have to ring the bell

and we sign them in. We have cameras that can see who is coming and going. He couldn't sneak in."

"That's good to know, thank you."

"You're welcome. Is there anything else I can help you with?"

"There is one more thing. Do you call Mark at his place of work ever? I mean, to help if Harriet is having a bad time?"

"We have done. Only once or twice in the whole eighteen months she's been here, though. We don't make a habit of it. People have to earn a living and we don't want to get anyone the sack. Besides, it's our job to see she is okay. It's what they pay us for."

"I may send an officer to get the dates on which you have called him from you, at some point, if needed."

"Of course."

"Does he bring in clothes for his mum?"

Pam shook her head. "She came in with a load of clothes. She has had no new things since then, not to my knowledge, anyway. We notice when our residents have something new."

"Well, you would, of course."

"Anything else I can help with?"

"Not at the moment, no. Thank you very much for the information." Yvonne handed her a card. "That's my contact details if you think of anything else."

As Yvonne walked away from Pant Glas, breathing deep of the salty air, she resolved to get Mark Bennett back in for questioning.

## 11

## TRUE OR FALSE?

"You lied to us, why?" Yvonne's face was a mask but there was an edge to her voice.

"I don't know what you mean." Mark Bennett continued to hold out.

"You told us you went AWOL from work because your mother's care home called you. You said they asked you to help as she was having a turn."

Mark blanched.

"What? You thought we wouldn't check? Did you think we would just take what you said at face value?"

His face puckered as though he wanted to cry. "Look, I'm not the bloke you're looking for, all right? What does it matter where I was? I wasn't at the seafront taking the life of a young woman. That's what matters. And you can't prove that I was because there will be no evidence. I wasn't there."

"We have you acting suspiciously on the morning she was murdered, hiding female clothing from your colleagues, and lying to us. You can see how this looks. What are we supposed to think?"

Mark stared at the desk.

"Why does it matter so much that you keep your whereabouts from us?"

"You wouldn't understand."

"Try me."

Mark shot a glance at the constable stood near the door.

Yvonne rose from her seat, walking over to the officer. "Sorry, could you give us a moment?"

"Certainly, ma'am."

Yvonne rejoined Mark Bennett. "So, what did you want to tell me?"

Mark coloured. "I'm transitioning. I've just started hormone treatment. I wear women's clothes in private and with very close friends. I don't steal the clothes. I haven't done that since I was younger, when I was too embarrassed to go into shops to buy them. Now, I can buy them online."

"Oh." Yvonne hadn't expected that. "Can anyone corroborate what you are saying?"

Mark took a letter out of his pocket. It was from a consultant regarding his next appointment.

"So, where were you Tuesday morning?"

"I went home to collect my boyfriend and see him off at the station. He lives and works in Shrewsbury, but had the Monday off. I had already said goodbye to him Monday night, just before leaving for my shift, but I had the urge to see him again before he went. I usually only see him every other weekend. Sometimes I go to stay with him. Two weeks can seem like forever."

"What's his name?"

"Stephen."

"Stephen what?"

"Yates."

"You know we can request CCTV from the station so, if you are lying-"

"Go ahead. I'll be on the camera. It's where I was. You'll see us hugging. It's hard, only seeing him every two weeks. Every other Friday, I have the highest of highs. But, on the Sunday, I have the lowest of lows. I am on a rollercoaster."

"Can you not move in together?"

"I would love to, but Stephen isn't ready. He gets embarrassed. His family don't know and their potential reaction terrifies him. Me, I only have my mother and she wouldn't know the difference."

"I see." Yvonne felt for him and his difficult situation. "We'll check out your story, but do me a favour?"

"What's that?"

"Don't lie to me again."

He nodded. "I won't."

∽

CHLOE GARSFORTH HEADED for the door of the lecture hall, having purposely sat at the back so that she could be one of the first out. Today was not one she wanted to spend hanging around, even in the queue to leave lectures. And the room was full from the top, all the way down its fairly steep slope, to the bottom. Hardly a seat empty.

"Chloe, could you hold on a minute?" It was the lecturer, Keith Griffiths.

She sighed, turning around to spot him running up the aisle steps towards her.

"Sorry, I wanted to speak to you about the essay you handed in. Do you have time to pop to my office?" He appeared a little dishevelled, his hair ruffled from hand-combing and he had loosened his tie as soon as the lecture finished.

Chloe looked at her watch.

"It won't take more than two minutes, I promise." He tilted his head, giving her doggy eyes.

"All right. As long as you're sure it won't take long."

"Great."

As she followed him along the corridor where the tutors rooms nestled, she wondered what it was like to have achieved tenure, to know you had a university lectureship for the rest of your life or as long as you wanted it. She had considered it before. Fancied it for herself. However, she lacked self-belief as regards achieving it. She wasn't one of those who had the next twenty years mapped out, to include jobs, marriage, children and mortgage, not necessarily in that order.

"Right." He cut through her thoughts as they reached his room. "It's here somewhere." He ran a hand over the various papers on his desk. "Ah, here you are, Chloe Garsforth." He needlessly read her name on the top.

"Did I pass it?" She asked with a frown.

"You did, but-"

"But?"

"Only just, I'm afraid. You didn't quote enough from source material. Your arguments are good but you've got to base them in precedent and you need to be quoting those precedents. Regularly."

"Oh, okay." She pursed her lips.

"I'm happy for you to re-write and submit, if you like. I'll hold off putting the mark in your file until you do."

"Really? Is that usual?"

"You're a special case."

She grimaced. "That's lame."

"Seriously, I see your potential."

"You do?"

"I do. You just lack the confidence you need to see it for yourself."

"I-"

He leaned towards her, putting his hand out against the doorframe, blocking her exit. "I tell you what, why don't I buy you a drink later? We can discuss it, then."

She could see dandruff, like snow, on the shoulders of his jacket. Hit with the stench of stale sweat and cigarettes, she only just stifled a gag. "That is not-"

"One drink. What harm could it do? You need a boost and I need relaxation. I tell you what, it could even be dinner. I've only got a microwave meal waiting for me. My Ex-wife used to do the cooking. I wish I'd learned, but I didn't."

*Really? Are you playing the vulnerable one?* Chloe shook her head. "Not tonight. I can't, I've made plans."

"Tomorrow, then? Go on. An hour, or two. What's the harm?"

Her heart thumped in her chest. She needed out of there. "Okay, tomorrow."

He dropped his arm. "Great. I'll give you a lift. Meet me at the top car park at seven."

She nodded, biting her lip.

"See you then." He could not control the grin on his face.

Chloe had the urge to change her mind, but was afraid. She wasn't sure why.

## 12

## A KILLER'S HAUNTS

The morgue was quiet, most of the staff having gone home.

Roger Hanson was in the middle of washing his hands when the DI arrived.

He wiped them before grabbing a file from the desk in the corner. "He stuffed her bra down her throat." He handed her his report. "But I believe you'd already guessed that, from what you said in your email?"

Yvonne nodded. "It was the only item missing from her clothing and I know the killer's signature. He took a risk with this one, though, didn't he? Down there on the seafront? It couldn't have been long before it got light. It's not exactly dead down there at sunup."

"There are no cameras there, though, are there?"

Yvonne shook her head. "No, unfortunately not."

"Well, I'm guessing he felt safe enough before it got light, wearing dark clothing, and there are several routes to escape from there on foot. Plenty of rabbit runs. He knew he could get away if he needed to."

She sighed. "Yes. What about sexual activity? Did you find any evidence?"

"Have a guess?" He nodded towards the report, tilting his head, scrutinising her face.

"Condom?"

"Right. As before, the victim could have had consensual sex any time in the last twenty-four to forty-eight hours, that's for you to investigate. If her killer raped her, either he did so after her death or she put up no resistance. There was no bruising to her inner thighs or to her pubic bone and no vaginal damage or bruising. She fought with him before her death, however, so a rape without resistance while she was still alive? Unlikely. Actually, I would venture, impossible."

"I see." Yvonne cast her eyes over the now-covered body on the morgue trolley. "How long do you think she was aware of what was happening?"

He pursed his lips, narrowing his eyes. "Several minutes? I'd say ten at the outside, based on the evidence. He couldn't keep her alive too long if he wanted to rape her after death. That would be a risk too far."

Yvonne nodded. "Thanks for this, Roger." She waved the report in the air. "I'll call you if I have any more questions."

"Sure."

∽

THE LIGHT FADED FAST, as did any heat the sun had conjured from the cold winter sky. There would be a deep frost tonight. Yvonne could feel the beginnings of it biting into her neck, ears and the end of her nose.

She pushed her hand into Tasha's, as they headed through the gateway between the Castle and the top of

Great Darkgate Street, delighting in its warmth. The heat travelled the length of her arm to her heart, and she smiled.

Tasha looked at her, grinning back. "So, DI Giles, we're here. Want to walk me through it?"

Yvonne's smile faded as she visualised Alice Brierley's death scene. "They found Alice here." She pointed to the pavement. "Her head lay towards the wall, her feet in the gutter, there. She was naked, and he'd dumped her clothing near her feet, along with a tie he used to gag her."

"DNA on the tie?"

Yvonne shook her head. "Nothing. We think he bought the tie for the purpose and he used gloves. Likely, he removed it from the packaging not long before using it on her. That's a point..." She hesitated.

"What?"

"Why gag her? He didn't gag the other two. So, why Alice?"

"Do you think he caught up with her down the road and manhandled her to somewhere he felt was safer for him?"

"Yeah, I do. It couldn't have been too far down the road. She fought back. Put up a hell of a fight, actually. He broke her arm while subduing her. Here, it's unlikely anyone would have heard her. But down the road, people were still about."

"Perhaps he kept her alive for a while, because she fought back, a punishment before dispatching her. Didn't you say you think he's a necrophiliac?"

"I suspect that he is, yes."

"So, his goal was to kill and rape her. But, if he's mad, maybe he gags her and tells her what he will do to her. Maybe, he relishes the conversion of her anger into fear."

"But he had the tie with him already."

"Maybe he bought a new tie and kept it in his pocket.

There's no saying he bought it specifically to use on a victim."

Yvonne pressed her lips together in thought. "That's true, I guess."

"He's one mean mother. So, you don't have DNA from any of these victims? They fight back, but no skin under fingernails? Anything like that?"

"No. We have fibres. We have fibres on the clothing of all three victims and on the bodies of two victims. But they don't match across the victims."

"So, wearing different outfits each time."

"Yes."

"And, I bet they are things bought for the purpose, perhaps from charity shops. He'll discard or burn them after each kill."

"Hmm. There's something else I wanted to ask you about."

"Go on."

"Well, all three victims struggled with him. He jumps them so, in theory, he could hit them with something to incapacitate or kill them right away. After all, if I am right, and he wants to rape them after death, he need not get into a scrap with them. So, why does he? What does fighting with them do for him?"

Tasha tilted her head. "Heightens his arousal, I'd say. I'd put money on that. Helps him get an erection. Maybe, he can't get one without it."

"Then there is the underwear. He stuffs an item of the girl's underwear down her throat after death. So far, he has used different underwear after each kill. With Alice, it was a sock. Kathy, her pants, and Amanda, her bra."

"Underwear has a particular significance for him, then.

And, he's baiting you guys. A little game he is tagging on — guess what item I will use next?"

"Well, he is out of options, now, isn't he?"

"If he kills again, and he will if he can, he will find something else to use, even if he has to tear it from a larger piece of clothing. Or, he could continue randomising items of underwear."

Yvonne shook her head. "I can't let him kill again, Tasha. I have to find him."

"You said he left the first victim in a rock pool?" Tasha took Yvonne's hand once more, ready to continue their walk.

"Yes." Yvonne pointed as they made their way towards town. "She would have come from that direction." She pointed to their right towards the junction of Bridge Street and Great Darkgate Street. "She crossed the main road and two shop CCTV cameras captured her as she walked along there." she pointed to their left. "That's Pier Street."

"Is that the way we are going?" Tasha asked.

"Yes."

They walked Pier Street until they could see the pier itself across the road.

"So, she walked along here and her intention was to turn right, towards Carpenter, her hall of residence. She had room number one, on the ground floor, with a view of the sea."

"And she never arrived."

"No. So somewhere around here, she met her killer and ended up going left, instead of right, and down towards the rock pools. Or, he took her across the road to the beach and killed her somewhere further along."

Tasha looked around them. "If she put up a fight here, someone would have heard. He persuaded her to go with him. Was she gagged?"

"Not that we know of, and they found no gag with the body."

"So, he persuaded her to walk with him. Used some excuse. Played on the goodness of her nature to help him. Perhaps, he told her he'd lost something, or someone?"

"I don't know, she was a bright girl..."

"Wait, do you think he knew them? Maybe, they knew and trusted him."

"That thought occurred to me. I have the team looking into connections between the girls. The obvious one is the university. All were on different courses, but they were all students."

"Okay, so you could look at members of university staff, or someone else that they are likely to have seen as students. Someone they wouldn't suspect as a person who would want to cause them harm."

"Like security? Or staff?"

"Right. Someone in a position of trust."

"Or, he had a weapon. He didn't use it, but it was enough to bring them under control."

"Yes, another possibility."

"He left kathy in a rock pool, just down there." Yvonne pointed. "Naked and looking out to sea. They found her pants in her throat. Not the way you would want to end your birthday. A university lecturer who was out walking his dog discovered her."

They looked at each other.

"You don't think he-"

Yvonne breathed deeply. "Hmm, I had an odd feeling about him. Perhaps, I should talk to Doctor Keith Griffiths, again."

"Right. What about victim three?"

"For Amanda Hartnett, we need to walk along the front

in the opposite direction. Come on." Yvonne led Tasha along the railings to their right.

They walked the full length of the promenade, past the band shelter and the children's play area, along past the old police station, and on to the kicking bar, below Constitution Hill cliffs.

"She lay there." Yvonne pointed to the area which was still cordoned off, the tent having been removed some time ago.

Tasha looked at the buildings towering above. "Surely someone saw something?"

Yvonne shook her head. "No-one in Alexandra Hall saw anything. All were fast asleep after a late-night party which went on into the small hours the night before, apparently, and the old police station is unoccupied. There are houses up behind Alexandra but they don't have a view through to the crime scene. Officers have been all along this part of the front and come up with nothing."

"Do you think he knew about the party?" Tasha frowned.

"I don't know. Could have been a stroke of luck on his part. We think his victim was jogging somewhere along here when she encountered him. Amanda's best friend said she liked to jog when it was getting light and she was in sports clothing. Except, when we found her, she was minus the clothing. The killer had stuffed her bra down her throat after her death. We think he may have had sex with her body, wearing a condom."

"Wow, that was brazen."

"Yes, and would have taken several minutes. Add that to the time taken to subdue and kill her and we are talking ten minutes, at least. And still no-one saw anything. Granted it was foggy, again, but I don't remember it being that thick a fog."

"It's like a part of him wants to get caught." Tasha scratched her head. "Or enjoys the risk of getting caught. You know, it is possible he doesn't want to kill. When he relieves the urge, he may feel disgusted at what he has done. Self-disgust is not that unusual in these cases. But, he's got a taste for death now. He will keep getting urges until you catch him."

"We've put out advisories for young females to stick to groups and not walk anywhere alone late at night. I hope they take heed. We've got more uniformed patrols out but they can only stretch so far. At least, for the moment, he appears to be remaining in the Aberystwyth area. If he moves further afield, we may really struggle with manpower."

"I suspect he'll stay within the Aber area, Yvonne."

"Yeah?"

"Yes. He seems to like students. He'll stay where he has the most likelihood of getting one. If he is finding victims opportunistically, he has got to stay within areas that have the highest density of targets."

"Of course." The DI nodded. "Thank you for coming with me on this macabre tour." She smiled at Tasha, placing her hand into the psychologist's once more. "I knew you would help organise my thoughts."

"You're welcome." Tasha pulled her in for a long hug. "You're cold. Let's go back to the Hotel."

## 13

## DEPARTURES

Chloe Garsforth waited for Hannah Martin to catch her up.

"What's the rush?" Hannah asked, still catching her breath.

"It's that lad I told you about, Adam Hardy."

"What about him?"

"He's at it again, look." She pointed to where Adam was walking backwards in front of two girls. The hunched body language of the latter, betrayed their discomfort.

"I feel like saying something."

Hannah shook her head, placing a hand on her friend's shoulder. "Don't. From what you've told me, and what I can see myself, I think he may have something like Asperger's. If so, he's bound to act a little different, but it's not something he can help. He probably doesn't see himself the way others do. I think he is just trying to be friendly and doesn't realise he is over the top."

"Right." Chloe grimaced, not convinced.

Hannah paused. "I tell you what, let's go invite him for a drink."

"What?"

"Sure, why not? We'll ask him if he wants to go to a bar and make it plain that a drink is all he can expect. He won't feel such an outcast and we will get to know him better. If we try, others may do so, too. Come on, I hate to see people left out. It's not right. There's two of us. I doubt he'll be any threat."

Chloe chewed her lower lip, thinking about it. "Okay, if you think it is a good idea. We'll let the others know what we are planning, just in case."

∽

THE BAR WAS QUIET, a substantial proportion of the student population having already departed the town for their parents' homes at various locations around the country. Soon, Chloe and Hannah would go too. This was their last week at halls.

Adam agreed to meet them for a drink at a bar on Pier Street. When they arrived, he was already there, drinking a pint at the bar.

"What you having, Chloe?" Hannah asked.

"I'll have a Gin and tonic, please."

"Two G&T's." Hannah called to the barman.

Adam joined them. "All right?" He asked, louder than was necessary.

Hannah rubbed her ear. "Yeah, we're good thank you. Glad you could make it for a drink. Just so you know, that's all it is. We wanted to have a chat and a drink. That's it. Okay?"

He frowned, contemplating this for a moment. "Yeah, sweet." He grinned.

"Good."

Chloe stared at Hannah, admiring the fact her friend could easily handle things. She knew what to say and was calm, but firm, with a sense of purpose that put others at ease. She did all this while ensuring boundaries were in place. It was quite a skill. Chloe wished she had it.

"Where you from, Adam?" Hannah asked, carrying the drinks as they seated themselves on metal barstools.

"Bristol," Adam answered, leaning on the bar and stretching his arm across to hold on to the opposite ledge.

"Bristol? I have family down there. One of my aunts and two cousins."

"Sweet." Adam grinned. "I bet I know them."

Hannah raised an eyebrow. "Bristol is a big place. You probably don't."

"I know everyone in Bristol," he asserted.

"Do you like living in Wales?" Hannah took a sip of her drink, wondering if this was such a good idea afterall.

"I do, now." He moved closer to them, along the bar.

Chloe, seated between Hannah and Adam, could feel his breath on her neck. She cleared her throat and pushed her stool back.

Hannah flicked her a glance. "Chloe, would you like to swap places with me, I can't quite hear what Adam is saying."

Chloe smiled her gratitude. "No problem."

They swapped places and Adam sat back on his stool as though realising that Hannah wouldn't stand for him breathing on her.

They continued swapping small-talk for a while, until two drink rounds later, Hannah and Chloe got up to leave.

"Come to my place?" Adam asked. "I've got vodka."

Chloe looked at her watch. "No, thank you, Adam. We've

got to get going. I'm going home to my family tomorrow and I still haven't finished packing."

As she and Hannah continued walking towards the door, Adam moved forward to block it.

"One drink. That's all I'm asking." There was a perceptible slur on his words.

Hannah put out her hand as a warning. "No. We are leaving, Adam. It was nice talking to you, but we have to go."

He lunged at her, pushing her back,. The bar staff came out from behind the bar.

"All right. All right, I'm going." He threw a look of disgust in their direction. "I'm bored, anyway."

∞

"You see?" Chloe flicked a glance behind as they walked away. "I told you what he's like. He's impossible."

"I'm fairly sure he is on the spectrum." Hannah sighed. "I don't think he can help the way he is. He doesn't read people's reactions or emotions very well. It must frustrate him."

"Are you always this understanding?" Chloe asked with a grin.

"I try."

"Well, I am secretly very impressed."

Hannah laughed. "Well, thanks. Come on, let's get back to halls."

∞

The morning briefing was about to start.

Yvonne skimmed through her notes, clarifying her

thoughts while Dewi fiddled with the laptop he would use to show the slides on the interactive whiteboard.

In front of them, the expectant faces of Sarah and Ifan, pens and notepads at the ready.

"Good morning everyone." Yvonne smiled, her eyes scanning her team. "I thought we'd start with any new information we have, so we can merge it before moving on. Can we start with you, Dewi?"

"Yes, ma'am." Dewi took the floor, pressing play on the laptop's remote. "Okay, I got the relevant CCTV from the rail station for the morning of Amanda Hartnett's death. I've screen-captured the frames we are interested in. It shows Mark Bennett walking along the platform next to a younger male. Bennett says something to the male and, as you'll see in the next several frames, they hug, before the male gets onto the train. They wave at each other and the train pulls out. The time-stamp reads five-fifty am. Bennett lingers on the platform for several minutes after the train has gone, looking in the direction it disappeared. He doesn't leave the station until just after six."

"That would support what he said to me regarding seeing his boyfriend Stephen Yates off."

"Right." Dewi agreed.

"However, although we see them walking along the platform together, we don't know what time Bennett got there, neither do we know where he went afterwards. In theory, there was a twenty-to-thirty minute window either side of this time, when Bennett could have been at the sea front hurting and murdering Amanda Hartnett." Yvonne tapped her pen on her hand.

"Timing would be tight, though, wouldn't it? I mean, it would take a good ten minutes to get from the station to the murder site, even if Bennett ran all the way. If he walked, I doubt he could do it. And the railway station CCTV did not capture his numberplate. If he used his car, he parked it elsewhere."

"Could you do me a favour, Ifan? Could you go down there and check out the times yourself? Walking and running, please. Bennett's car never left the hospital carpark. I confirmed that with the warden, yesterday."

Ifan nodded. "Will do, ma'am."

"Dewi, can we see about finding Stephen and talk to him about his relationship with Bennett? Bennett was reluctant to give me details about Stephen, but he's got to if he wants to use his boyfriend as an alibi. I think it likely Mark Bennett is innocent but we wouldn't be doing the victims justice if we left any stone unturned."

The DI continued. "It's very possible these girls knew their killer and trusted him. Kathy Swales may have willingly walked some distance with him before her murder. So, Sarah and Ifan, I'd like you to expand on the work Dewi has been doing regarding sex offenders. I'd like you to look at the university staff. All grades. See whether any have history of offences against females, to include both convicted and alleged sexual assault. Include offences that may have been plea-bargained down from sexual assaults to assault. Any voyeuristic offences could also be relevant. Use your judgement. There may be cases that were dropped prior to, or during, court hearings. As you know, some sexual offences don't result in the offender going onto the register so you'll have to dig. If anyone comes into the above categories, we'll look at them further. Okay? Notes any offences against students. Listen out for rumours about staff. Have female students complained of anyone pestering them? If so, check the pest out and let me know. Happy with that?"

Both DCs agreed.

Yvonne smiled at them. "Okay, next to fibres. Dewi, if you'll do the honours."

"Certainly, ma'am." Dewi flicked the projector back on. "They extracted fibres from the clothing of the dead girls."

Images of the fibres appeared on the screen.

"They think the black fibres at the top of the slide are from a woollen jumper. They found them on Kathy Swales's clothing. There were no fibres of this type on the clothing of subsequent victims. The dark brown fibres are cotton ones, found on Alice Brierley. Forensics believe them to be from a cotton-mix jacket. The third set of fibres are from a cotton tie. They found fragments of it between Alice's teeth. The only DNA on that tie has proven to be Alice's. We do not believe the offender ever wore that tie. We think he bought it for use on his victim. It is possible he stole the garments."

Dewi glanced at them all before continuing. "He may buy new clothes, prior to dispatching each of his victims. Meaning, if we catch him, we may not find matching items in his wardrobe. However, we should still keep an eye out for a suspect wearing clothes similar to those described. It's clear he prefers dark clothing when he attacks. We need to bear this in mind."

Dewi continued. "There will be a news conference for the public tomorrow, when we will disclose the clothing we are interested in. See if it rings any bells with the public."

"Questions?" Yvonne asked.

The others shook their heads.

"Okay, then. Let's get to it."

## 14

## COLLEGE TROUBLES

"What have got for me?" Yvonne leaned back as she sat at her desk. She could see the excitement in Sarah and Ifan's eyes and knew it had to be something important.

"You want to tell her?" Ifan asked Sarah.

She gave him a grin and began reading from her notes. "Okay… First up, John Lloyd. He's a member of the university security team. Been on their staff for seven years. There was a disciplinary hearing two years ago, and he came close to prosecution."

"What for?" Yvonne leaned forward, her gaze, intense.

"Alleged sexual assault."

"Really?"

"Yeah, apparently there had been a fracas between two girls in the student bar. Nothing serious, but John Lloyd stepped in to break it up and make sure it didn't get nasty."

"Okay…"

"Afterwards, one girl alleged he had touched her breast and slapped her on the buttocks."

"So, what happened at the disciplinary? And how did he avoid prosecution?"

"Lack of evidence. He denied it. There was no CCTV of the incident and no witnesses for what the girl alleged happened."

"So she could have made it up? What was the girl's name?"

"Helen Edwards."

"Is she still at the university?"

"She is, ma'am. She's in her third year, studying English."

"Then she is someone I would definitely like to speak to. What was the outcome of John Lloyd's disciplinary hearing?"

"They put him back on six months' probationary period, ma'am." Sarah pushed stray behind her ear.

"Interesting. That suggests to me that the university didn't entirely believe John Lloyd's version. I think Dewi and I will pay him a visit. Good work, Sarah and Ifan. Good work."

Ifan took over the telling, puffing out his chest. "There's another character you might find interesting ma'am. In fact, I think you spoke to him. He found the body of Kathy Swales."

"Doctor Keith Griffiths?"

"Yes, ma'am. Instead of calling him a lecturer, as I understand it, the ladies refer to him as the leacher-er."

Yvonne stifled a grin. "Good to see the girls have a sense of humour."

"According to the student rep, Griffiths has a reputation for chasing after female students. He has asked several out on dates and received a warning for his conduct. Apparently, he told a colleague in front of several girls at a disco, that whereas other male lecturers go to bed with an ache in their balls, he doesn't have to, because girls are nice to him."

"He said what?"

"You heard that right, ma'am."

"Good God, what on earth is he still doing teaching there?"

"Again, when the vice chancellor asked questions, Griffiths denied saying it. Oh, and there is something else."

"Go on..."

"According to the same student rep, Keith Griffiths knew Kathy Swales. He reckoned Kathy had complained that Griffiths made inappropriate remarks, during conversations with her, when she was in the outside smoking area having a cigarette. He smokes too, apparently. Again, she claimed he gave her unwanted attention and she felt uncomfortable, but the rep could not remember specifics."

"Well, I know much of this is hearsay, but I think we should investigate. I wanted to speak to Griffiths again, anyway. Something my psychologist friend said to me the other day got me thinking about him. Thank you, both of you. I will interview these men as soon as possible."

Sarah and Ifan gave each other a high five.

∼

LUCKILY FOR THE TEAM, Helen Edwards was still in Aberystwyth until three days before Christmas. She and her boyfriend rented a flat in the Waunfawr district of the town and planned to go to both sets of parents for Christmas and New Year.

Helen agreed to go at the station and Yvonne met her in reception.

Yvonne held her hand out to the athletic young woman who stood as she entered. "Helen Edwards?"

"Yes. That's me." She straightened her shoulder-length auburn hair and walked over to shake Yvonne's hand.

"Thank you for coming in at such short notice. I understand my sergeant explained to you what it was about?"

"Yes, he did. I have to say it surprised me, the police contacting me now, two years after the assault. It didn't do me much good when I complained last time."

"I'm sorry about that." Yvonne pursed her lips. "Please take a seat," she offered, as they entered the interview room.

"Thanks. It wasn't the police's fault. The officers who spoke to me were lovely, and they did their best to take it forward. But, I'd been drinking heavily on the night it happened and there was no independent corroboration of what I was alleging. I think my assailant knew that and took full advantage."

"Would you like to tell me what you believe happened?"

Helen pulled a face. "What I *believe* happened? I don't *believe* it happened, I *know* it happened. I may have had a few drinks but I know what I saw and felt."

"Talk me through it from the beginning." Yvonne's voice was soft. "What happened before the assault?"

Helen took a deep breath. "Well, I was drinking with my partner in the student bar. We were planning on leaving soon, so it was my last drink. My partner was talking to me and another girl came leaning on him, giving him the eye. Or, at least, that's how I read it. In my inebriated state, I took offence and told her to back off. I'm not usually argumentative but, like I say, I was worse for wear."

"What happened then?"

"She told me to mind my own business. That she had every right to stand where she was and why was I so possessive? Or words to that effect. It was something and nothing, really, but we raised our voices and security came over. One officer took the other girl off to talk to her and John Lloyd wandered over to me and walked me off to the side, telling me to calm down. My partner, Steve, came to stand with me, but John Lloyd told him to back off and stay at the bar, that he was just calming me down. He had his back to the room, and I was behind him."

"So, he blocked you from your partner's view?"

"By that time, Steve was explaining to bar staff what was going on. So, yeah, he blocked me from view and Steve was looking the other way."

"What happened then?"

"Well, Lloyd asked me if I had any weapons on me or anything sharp. I told him no. He patted me down. I told him he had no right to do that, but he said I might be a risk. That's when he held my right breast. Only for a second, but that was a second too long. I pushed it off and, as I went to walk back to my boyfriend, he slapped me on the buttock. To be honest, his whole manner gave me the creeps. If I hadn't been drunk and offended, I might have been afraid."

"I see." Yvonne frowned. "Have you ever heard of John Lloyd treating women like that before? Or since?"

"Not like that, but I have heard of him trying to chat to girls as they walked down Penglais Hill, getting overly friendly."

"Has he ever approached you, since that time?"

"No, never. After risking prosecution last time, he is wary of me. He doesn't like me and never speaks, but that is fine. I wouldn't want him to acknowledge me. Im happiest if he stays far away from me. He knows what he did, Inspector. He knows full well. I'm only annoyed that he got clean away with it."

"I understand he had to do a fresh probationary period for his job."

"And that's it? It should have been a court hearing and conviction."

Yvonne tilted her head. "I'm glad our officers tried, at least."

"Why are you asking me this, anyway?" Helen narrowed her eyes. "Has he done something else?"

"We are looking into the backgrounds of several people in the Aberystwyth area."

"Wait, is this for the murder of those girls? Do you think it involved him?"

"We don't have a concrete suspect, as yet, but we are looking at all those who came into contact with the women."

"I hope you catch whoever did it, and soon. Everyone's jumpy. I'll be glad to get back to my parent's place. With most my friends gone, it will be lonely and scary to be out and about."

"We have more officers around the town." Yvonne gave a reassuring smile.

"I don't see that killer letting a little thing like that stop him." Helen grimaced. "I'm sorry, I didn't mean that. It's reassuring to know there are more officers about. I am appreciating how the women of White Chapel must have felt during Jack the Ripper's murderous reign."

Yvonne nodded. "Don't walk about on your own, especially after dark."

"Oh, don't worry, Inspector, I have no plans to wander about by myself."

Yvonne thanked Helen and saw her out of the station. She was loath to class John Lloyd as a firm suspect, but she could start by speaking to him about campus security and see what he had to say. *Shake the tree*, she thought.

～

HAVING SOUGHT the vice chancellor's permission to speak to the security guard, Yvonne found the latter in the hut at the campus' gateway.

He waved her in when she flashed her badge at him, pointing to a small carpark to the right, just downhill from where he was.

She drove down into it, thankful that there were still places available. She parked in the nearest space and walked back up to the security box.

Lloyd was straightening his cap, bending his knees to look into a small mirror he had taped to the cabin frame.

"I shouldn't bother, it won't impress me," Yvonne muttered, sighing just out of earshot. She wore a trouser suit, and no way was she going to straighten anything.

"Inspector Giles?" he asked, as she reached the box.

"Yes, Yvonne Giles."

A car came to the entrance. He waved it through. "John Lloyd. You want to speak to me about campus security?"

"Yes, is that all right?"

"Of course." He smirked. "You've come to the expert."

"Well, that's good to know."

The box was small. Too small. It didn't feel right being in such a confined space with him. "I thought you were finishing your shift about now?"

He looked at his watch. "I am. I'm waiting for my colleague to get here for the changeover. He drives in from Talybont. He's sometimes late."

"I see. We can wait for him to get here, that's fine by me."

He shrugged. "Whatever suits."

Yvonne prayed the colleague would be there sooner rather than later. "Have you always been in security?"

He shook his head. "I started out as a butcher's apprentice. I wasn't very good at presentation."

Yvonne stared at him. "Is that why you changed to this?"

He shook his head. "No, I wanted to be a security guard. I always enjoyed the gym. I'm a big guy. This suits me better."

"All right, John?" The colleague had arrived.

"Mal, glad you could make it," Lloyd chided, looking at his watch.

"Sorry, mate. Got held up."

"No worries. Don't do it again." He winked at the DI.

She stifled a cringe.

"We can talk at the Arts Centre, if you like. I usually get a sandwich there after my shift." Lloyd pointed up towards the buildings on the left.

Yvonne knew where the Arts Centre was, having been frequently with Tasha. "Great. We'll go there."

They walked up the incline towards the Arts Centre steps; the DI relieved to be out of the security cabin.

The Arts Centre was busy. John Lloyd went to the cafe counter to get a sandwich.

Yvonne wasn't hungry. She waited in the queue to get a coffee. The caffeine might give her an edge.

"So, what did you want to know?" he asked, as they grabbed the last free table.

"How many are their in your team?"

"Altogether? Four. Myself, Mal, Kate and Tom."

"Okay. Are you always on duty at the entrance to the campus?"

He shook his head. "No, I sometimes do night patrols,

walking around campus with one of my colleagues, and sometimes I am on reception."

"Are female students safe on campus?"

"I would say so. We are a hard-working team. We do our best to ensure everyone's safety."

"I see. I understand there was an incident two years ago, when someone accused you of assault?" She scrutinised his face.

He sighed, a look of disgust on it. "I thought I'd put all that behind me. Look, after a few drinks, some females get hysterical. There was a heated argument going on between two girls over a guy. It looked to be about to kick off, so myself and a colleague intervened. I got accused of groping the girl I talked to. She was off her head. The most I did was to hold her back so she couldn't get to the other girl. I had to go to court over it. They dropped the case through lack of evidence. That's because I did nothing. There were enough people around who would have seen it if I had."

"Do you ever approach any of the girls on campus?"

"What? What is this?" The colour had risen in his cheeks, his body tensed. "What's the real reason you are questioning me?"

"You know we have had several murders of young women in Aberystwyth the last few months?"

"Yes, of course I do, but what's it to do with me?"

"I'd like to know what safety measures are in place to protect students on site."

"Oh." He frowned, calming down. "We are patrolling more regularly and for longer. The university are giving out advisories to female students warning them not to walk alone after dark and to keep friends informed of where they are. You can't control their movements, so you do the best you can to keep them informed. We check the credentials of anyone coming onto campus that we do not recognise and one thing the patrols look out for is pedestrians who shouldn't be here."

"I see." Yvonne nodded. "That's fine."

"Is that it?" he asked, eyes narrowed.

"Yes, that answers my question." She finished her coffee and rose to leave. "Thank you for your time." She held out her hand to shake his.

"No problem," he answered, but he didn't accept the handshake.

"Make sure those girls are safe," she called, as she walked away.

∾

KEITH GRIFFITHS' office was a room of barely organised mess. Papers littered the desk, the cupboards, and lay piled high on the floor on one side of his desk chair. The waste paper bin needed emptying and the jacket hanging on the back of the door reeked of stale cigarette smoke.

He took a lever arch file off the chair on her side of the desk so she could sit.

"Thank you." She wasn't sure she wanted a seat amongst the dust and mayhem, but accepted it despite her reservations.

"Sorry, it gets chaotic in here. I know where everything is. It just looks like I don't."

She nodded. "Busy man."

He shrugged. "Everyone wants to study law. How can I help you?" he asked, running a hand through hair that needed grooming.

She pointed to the body camera on her jacket. "This is running. Do you mind?"

"You're recording this?"

"We wear body cameras a lot, these days. Is it a problem?"

He shook his head.

"There are some things I needed to clarify with you, if I may?"

"Sure..." He shrugged. "If I can help, I will."

"When I spoke to you last time, you mentioned having touched Kathy Swales' body."

"That's right, I did." He leaned back in his chair.

"You said she felt cold, and that was how you knew she was dead."

"It was the confirmation I needed, yes." He narrowed his eyes.

"We checked Kathy's body for prints and didn't find any. You said you touched her upper arms. There were no prints on her upper arms."

He pursed his lips, leaning forward and placing his hands together as though praying, resting his chin on his fingertips, elbows on the desk. "So, what are you saying? That I didn't touch her? I'm fairly sure I wore gloves. Yes, Yes, I did. I wore gloves."

"Then how did you know she was cold?" Yvonne tilted her head.

"She was like ice. I felt her through the gloves. Try it for yourself. Touch the inside of your freezer with gloves, you'll still feel it. We'd had the first frost of the year. She'd probably been on the beach for most of the night. Add to the cold temperature, the extra wind chill off the sea, and you have your explanation."

The DI nodded. "Do you still have the gloves?"

He shook his head. "No, I'm afraid I don't."

This time, it was Yvonne who narrowed her eyes. "Where are they?"

"I lost them."

"When? Where?"

"A few weeks ago, while I was out walking Benji. I think they must have fallen out of my pocket when I pulled out a bag to gather Benji's poop. I couldn't remember exactly where that was, but it was likely somewhere along the beach."

"You didn't go back to find them?"

He pulled a face. "They're gloves. They're not the family heirlooms."

"I see."

"I didn't realise you would want me to produce them. Where is this going, Inspector? Do you think I had something to do with Kathy's death?"

"Like I said, Doctor Griffiths, I needed clarification. You told me you didn't know Kathy."

"I didn't."

"She told a friend you smoked cigarettes with her."

"Did I? Well, I might have. I smoke. If there are students or staff in the smoking area, I make conversation. It's lonely, and cold, if all you do is smoke on your own. It's called socialising. I didn't realise it was an offence."

Yvonne sighed. "Obviously, it is not an offence to socialise, but you said you didn't know her, when clearly you did."

"I don't remember all the faces I see. I have never taught her. I didn't even know her name until after her death."

"Do you remember smoking with her, now I've reminded you?"

"Vaguely."

"She told a friend you made her feel uncomfortable."

"Right, that's it. You can turn that camera off and leave my office. If you want to discuss anything further, you must do it with a solicitor present. I don't like where this is going, Inspector. I think you are trying to lead me places. I don't know what your agenda is, but I am unhappy with your line of questioning." He rose from his seat and held the door open.

"Very well, Doctor Griffiths. Thank you for talking to me. I will let you know if I need to know anything further. If I do, I will call you in for a formal interview."

"You do that." His expression chilled her, his pupils were so large they made his eyes appear black.

She was glad to see the back of his office.

## 15

## UNFAMILIAR TERRITORY

When Yvonne returned to the office, Dewi made her a brew.

"How did it go with Lloyd and Griffiths?" he asked, handing her a hot mug.

"I have to confess, Dewi, I am not a fan of either of them."

"But, are they murderers?"

"Lloyd fancies himself as a ladies' man, I think. He's vain and, I suspect, he's probably a hit with many young women. However, I think he assumes that every woman he comes into contact with will come under his spell and is probably surprised when they don't. I think him being capable of committing the assault Helen Edwards alleged, but murder? I don't really think he is capable of that. I just don't see it. He should stay on the suspect list, for now, but he is low down on the list, based on what I have observed."

"Okay." Dewi scratched his head. "What about Griffiths?"

"Now, that guy gives me the creeps. There is something about him that rubs me the wrong way. I could see him persistently chasing females and I think he is hiding things. He claims to have lost the gloves he says he wore when he touched Kathy Swales to see if she was dead. He said he lost them while walking his dog. He is very good at thinking on his feet and is slippery as they come. I'm not convinced he is capable of murder, but there is something distasteful about him. Put it this way, if I had youngsters of university age, I wouldn't want him to be their tutor."

"He found Kathy's body, and both she and Amanda Hartnett were killed on his dog route."

"That's right. He had access to the girls, and he walks his dog where they found the bodies, but we could say that about others. He is high on my list of suspects. I don't think we have enough to justify a search of his home. I'd love access to his wardrobe for fibre comparison."

"Why don't you speak to our DCI? See what he thinks? Maybe it's enough that some students have flagged him as someone who has made them feel uncomfortable."

"We need something more concrete, Dewi. Can you dig into his background? See if there is anything criminal in his past. I may put a tail on him. Perhaps, Sarah and Ifan could keep tabs on him for a few days. We should be prudent. Whoever we show a major interest in will have the country's press camped out in their garden. That kind of mud sticks, even if they are proven innocent. You know that. Gather everything we have, forensically, and we'll plan our next moves."

"Yes, ma'am."

"Also, the sex offenders you have identified, talk to them even if they have cast iron alibis. They may have intel."

"Right."

At six-foot-one, Joel Davies stood a good six inches taller than Yvonne. He had agreed to come to the station rather than see police in his room in the hall of residence.

Dressed in jeans and a shirt, his short-cropped hair appeared to have had a trim recently. He yawned, taking a seat and rubbing the bags under his eyes.

"Thank you, for coming in, Joel. I'm Yvonne Giles."

"Is there any news?" he asked, his eyes scanning her face.

She shook her head. "Not yet, I'm afraid. I'm so sorry for your loss, Joel. We want to prevent this happening to anyone else, so I will gratefully receive any information you can give me today."

He nodded. "I will do anything to help you catch my girlfriend's killer. If I get my hands on him, I'll-"

She held up her hand. "I understand you're hurting, but please trust us to get justice for you. Don't take matters into your own hands."

He shrugged. "I just want him caught."

"I know." She cleared her throat. "I must warn you, some things I ask will concern private matters and may touch on sensitive subjects. Are you ready for that?"

"Yes."

"Joel, were you with Amanda during the night before she was murdered?"

"Yes, she stayed in my room with me."

"What time did she leave you?"

"Just after five. She was an early riser and liked to go for early morning runs. I'm not a morning person. It was one of the few things we didn't see eye-to-eye on."

"How was she, before she left?"

"Energetic." His mouth twitched in a half smile. "She

was ready to go. I was still in bed and wanting to go back to sleep."

"And did you?"

"What? Go back to sleep? Yes, yes, I did. I wish I'd gone with her but it would have been the first time. I'm not a jogger. I like team sports. I play rugby as a fly-half. I've never understood the appeal of running for running's sake, but I wish I had gone with her that morning."

"I know... Can I ask, were you intimate that night?"

He frowned, thinking for a moment. "No."

"Are you sure?"

"Yes, why?"

"When you were intimate, did you use protection?"

"Amanda was on the pill. That was all the protection we needed. We were solid. I had been thinking of asking her to marry me. We didn't sleep around and we didn't use any other protection."

"Not condoms?"

"No." His eyes narrowed. "Why? Did someone have sex with her using a condom? Did her killer-"

"I don't know." Yvonne said, truthfully. "Traces of spermicide were present and we have a suspicion the killer may have been responsible. I would ask you not to repeat that, for the time being, it could jeopardise the case."

"I understand. I won't say anything. I can't bear the thought of her going through that on top of everything else."

"If it helps, she may not have known much about it."

"I see." He put his head in his hands.

"Are you having counselling for your grief, Joel?"

He shook his head. "No. You're not the first person to suggest it. I just want to deal with this in my own way. She was the person I wanted to spend my life with. I wish I'd told her that."

"I'm sure she would have known the strength of your feelings." Yvonne tilted her head. "Us females are good at reading the signs."

"You think?" He raised his eyes to hers and she could tell he was hungry for thoughts like that. Took succour from them.

"Yes."

"I miss her."

"We will find her killer, Joel, and we will bring him to justice."

"You know, I believe you. You seem sincere." Joel smiled at her, though his eyes were sad.

"Thank you for coming to see us today." She shook his hand. "We'll keep you informed."

## 16

## AN UNEXPECTED ARREST

As the DI headed back to CID, Sarah met her in the corridor.

"Ma'am, they have arrested a youth for a prolonged assault on a female student at the castle. He hit her and dragged her by the hair. He is down in the cells. They found a lock knife on him."

"Did they? What's his name?"

"Adam Hardy. He is also a student, studying law, apparently."

"He's in Keith Griffiths' department?"

"I don't know."

"Can I see him?"

"I don't see why not? I'll let custody know to expect you."

"Thanks."

Though at first excited by the news, she didn't think a young student was responsible for the murders. His confidence would not be high enough. Still, stranger things had happened, and she needed to rule him out.

She gathered together the files needed and headed

down to the cells, speaking to the desk sergeant en route. "Hey, I hear you had someone brought in for assault?"

"Yes, about an hour ago. Adam Hardy. They have finished processing him, if you want to have a word."

"I do. Do you know if he had anything else on him besides a knife? Condoms for instance?"

The sergeant examined the charge sheet. "Chewing gum, his dorm keys, twelve-pounds eighty, and... oh yes, a condom. Just the one."

"One condom?"

"Yes. I believe they found it in a back pocket of his jeans. I'll come and unlock the cell for you."

"Thank you."

She followed the sergeant along to the cells and waited while he unlocked Adam Hardy's door.

She knocked before entering. "Adam?"

He jumped up from the built-in bed. "Get me out of here. I shouldn't be in here, I'm an agoraphobic."

She pulled a face. "Agoraphobia is a fear of open spaces, Adam. I should have thought you would prefer to be in a place like this if you suffered from that."

"Claustrophobia," he shouted. "I'm claustrophobic. You need to let me out."

"You didn't mention this to the officers who processed you and don't you live in halls? Your student room cannot be much bigger than this. This is a decent-sized cell."

He sat back on the bed, his arms folded. "I'm hungry."

"I'll ask the desk sergeant to organise food when I leave," she offered. "Would you like a hot drink as well?"

He nodded.

"Adam," she began. "Would you like to tell me why they arrested you?"

"I assaulted someone."

## Death in the Mist

She found his lack of eye contact disconcerting. "I know that. What I meant was, can you tell me why you committed the assault?"

"She was winding me up."

"The girl you assaulted?"

"Yes."

"In what way?"

"I offered her a chewing gum, and she said no."

"And that wound you up?"

"No, not that. I asked her if she wanted to go for a drink and I put my hand on her shoulder. She pushed it off."

"And that angered you?"

"I grabbed her arm and told her I was only being friendly. She told me to get lost. Called me a weirdo. I hate being called that, so I pushed her and she fell over. When she got up, she swung her bag at me so I punched her and grabbed her hair."

"I'm told you were dragging her by the hair."

"I was angry. I wanted to hurt her."

"Do you usually hurt girls, Adam?"

"Not usually. She made me mad. I wanted to hurt her." He gritted his teeth.

"You are aware you are under caution, Adam?"

"What's that?"

"An officer will have warned you that if you cannot answer questions, when asked, we could inform a court of your failure to cooperate."

"Oh, yeah."

"Okay. Do you have a girlfriend?"

He shook his head. "No. That's why I asked that girl to go for a drink."

"Do you always carry a condom around in your pocket?"

He lowered his head. "Yeah."

"Why is that?"

"In case I get lucky."

"Do you sometimes get lucky?"

He shook his head.

"Have you ever been lucky, Adam?"

"No."

"Officers will search your student room. Do you understand that?"

"Why?"

"They found you in possession of a blade. They'll want to ensure you have no more such items stashed away. Lock knives are offensive weapons. Have you asked for a solicitor?"

"No."

"Would you like one?"

"Yes."

"Very well. I will organise food and a hot drink and request a duty solicitor to be with you for a formal interview." She turned to leave.

"Will I be here long? I've got things to do. People to see. I'm a busy guy. Folks need me."

"We won't keep you longer than necessary, Adam. Once we have interviewed you, you will be charged with the assault and possession of an offensive weapon and released on bail, if appropriate."

She left him to think about his situation, wondering whether he might have something else going on with his mental health.

∼

THE DUTY SOLICITOR now accompanied Adam Hardy and

Yvonne was ready to interview him. She asked Dewi to go with her.

The DI introduced herself for the recording, inviting everyone else to do similar, then renewed the caution for Adam.

"Adam, you are aware we have arrested you for an assault on Tanya Burns, whereby you punched her to the body and dragged her by her hair."

"I didn't punch her, I pushed her hard."

"She alleges a punch, and she has a sizeable fresh bruise which would corroborate her story. In any event, a push is still considered an assault."

"She was rude to me."

"In what way was she rude to you, Adam?"

"Well, I asked her if she wanted some chewing gum and she said she didn't. So, I asked her if she would like to go for a drink with me. She wouldn't do that either."

"Is that why you hurt her? Because she wouldn't accept gum from you, a stranger, or go for a drink with you?"

"She told me to go away."

"Did you consider that it might scare her? Especially, if you were persisting after she had already said no?"

"She wasn't scared."

"How do you know she wasn't scared?"

"She sounded confident."

"People can fake confidence when they are feeling scared. Is that when you assaulted her?"

"No. She told me to fuck off."

"I see. Well, if she had already politely and then firmly turned you down, and it hadn't worked, perhaps she felt something more forceful might do the trick? I think many people would react the same way, if they felt uncomfortable or threatened."

"I didn't threaten her."

"I understand that, but your persistence may have felt threatening because the young woman did not know what your intentions towards her were."

He shrugged.

"Tell me about the knife."

"What about it?"

"Why did you have it on you?"

"Don't know."

"Did you intend using it?"

"No."

"Why do you carry it?"

"Because you don't know who's about."

"Do you always carry a knife?"

"Not always, I don't take them into class."

"So what scares you when you are out and about?"

"Lots of people get stabbed these days."

"Lots of people get stabbed with their own knives. Did you know that? If you go out with a knife, you are more likely to get hurt with one. That's a fact based on statistics."

"You don't know what I have had to put up with in life. They have bullied me since primary school."

"I am sorry you have suffered bullying, Adam, you know there is counselling available for people who are victims of bullying. We could refer you in for it?"

"That wouldn't protect me from being attacked, would it?"

"You study law, Adam. Surely, you above all people know better than to carry. Have you ever threatened anyone with the knife? Females, for instance?"

"No."

"You're sure?"

"Of course, I'm sure."

"Were you hoping to get lucky?"

"What?"

"You had a condom in your back pocket."

"His cheeks coloured as he hunched over and into himself, entwining the fingers of both hands."

Yvonne thought she saw a sheen of sweat on his forehead. "I'm sorry, Adam, I didn't mean to embarrass you."

"You think I'm a loser, don't you?"

"I can promise you that I don't think you are a loser."

"You think that no girl would want me."

"I don't think that at all. The right girl will want you, provided you go about asking her nicely and listen to what she has to say. If a girl says no, move on. If she says yes, you have yourself a date."

"I always carry a condom in case I need one."

"Have you used one recently?"

"No."

"Have you ever used one?"

"No."

"Have you ever had intercourse?"

"Hang on a minute, Inspector. My client does not have to answer that. How is it relevant to the charges? You can't charge him with being in possession of a condom. If you want to question him in connection with other matters, you have to put those to him and have good reason for doing so."

"Thank you for reminding me." Yvonne pursed her lips.

"Adam, did you know that three female students have been murdered in three months in Aberystwyth?"

"Yes."

"So, you will know why any assaults on females in the area, particularly if the attacker carries a weapon and a condom, will cause a lot of uncomfortable questions from us, and may place you on our suspect list."

"For murder?"

"Yes."

"Look, I pushed her and pulled her hair. She made me angry. It doesn't mean I wanted to kill her."

"You made yourself angry. You put yourself in her space when she was minding her own business. There is such a thing as taking responsibility for your own actions, Adam. You would do well to own the things you do."

"Have you been in trouble before, Adam?"

He shrugged. "I stole sweets from a shop when I was a kid. I got a fine for it."

"Anything else?"

"No."

"I have a printout here from our national database, it says you received a Youth Offending Order, aged thirteen, for seven counts of shoplifting."

"All right, I shoplifted when I was a child. I haven't done that for years. I have ADHD and Asperger's. I take Ritalin for my ADHD when it's bad. Happy?"

"That goes some way to explaining what happened, yes. Thank you for telling me. I will give you a leaflet, on your way out, for an excellent support group here in Aberystwyth. I suggest you call them and meet with them. They will help you with many, if not all, of the issues you face, such as forming new relationships. Is that okay?"

"Sure."

"All right. We will charge you for the offence of assault and I will advise our officers to caution you for possession of an offensive weapon. The knife will remain confiscated and, should you be caught in possession of one again, you will be prosecuted and face the consequences. As regards the assault, I am sure your solicitor will advise about informing the court of mitigating circumstances, such as your ADHD and Asperger's."

As she left, Yvonne couldn't help but feel sorry for him. It was clear he was desperate for female company but had no idea how to approach them. She hoped he would take her up on attending to the support group.

A team were on their way to search his room for items of clothing that might match the fibres found on the dead girls. Yvonne doubted they would find any, but she had been wrong before.

## 17

## THE ELUSIVE BOYFRIEND

Mark Bennett had agreed to see Yvonne, at the police station, before he started his late shift at the hospital.

Yvonne took him to an interview room. "Thank you for coming in to see me. I appreciate your time." She showed him to a seat.

"My shift starts in an hour," he said, looking at his watch.

"No problem, this shouldn't take long. Mark, we checked the railway station CCTV, and you were where you said you were."

"Of course I was." He frowned.

"You said the man you saw onto the train was your partner, Stephen Yates, is that correct?"

"Yes..." He narrowed his eyes. "Why?"

"Can you give me his address and contact details?"

"Why?"

"I don't mean to cause offence, but we only have your word for who he is, and that he is your partner. He could have been a friend or just someone you met at the railway station. The fact is, we now believe that Amanda Hartnett died in the hour before you saw that young man off. If he is your partner, and he stayed with you, we can speak with him and confirm him as your alibi. If, however, he is not your partner, and you were merely seeing him off, you could have committed murder before you went to the station."

"That's ridiculous."

"It probably is, but I wouldn't be doing my job properly if I didn't check it out. You appreciate that?"

"I don't have his address."

"What do you mean you don't have his address?"

"Like I told you before, he doesn't want his family to know his sexuality. He isn't out to anyone. He won't give me his address because he is afraid I might turn up at his house."

"You told me he lives in Shrewsbury."

"He does. I just don't know *where* in Shrewsbury."

"Do you know his birthday? Or his national insurance number?"

"No."

"How much of a partner is this guy?" She tilted her head. "You don't seem to know very much about him."

"I know enough."

"How did you two meet?"

"Grindr."

"So, on a dating website?"

"Yes."

"Do you know if Stephen Yates is even his real name?"

"I believe it is but if you are asking if I have proof that it is, no, I don't."

"When are you seeing him again?"

"I don't know."

"You don't know?"

"Well, he'll get in touch when he can come to my place again."

"And you don't go to see him?"

"Well, obviously not. I don't have his address."

"Do you not agree a next date when you see each other? I thought you saw each other fortnightly? This relationship seems a bit vague."

"Look, what is this?" He rose from his seat.

"When you see him again, could you ask him to call me so that I can meet him?" She held out her card.

"Why?"

"So I can verify your whereabouts on the morning of Amanda Hartnett's death."

He sighed. "Fine." He accepted her card.

"You know I wouldn't judge you if it were a one-night stand. I'm a big girl, I know people do such things."

He scowled at her. "He wasn't a one-night stand."

"Very well. Thank you for coming in. I will see you out."

∽

THE FOLLOWING DAY, Yvonne caught up with Ifan and Sarah in the incident room. "How are you doing? Have you traced Mark Bennett's boyfriend, Stephen Yates, yet?"

Sarah shook her head. "Not yet, ma'am. We've done the Shrewsbury phonebook and found several Stephen Yates. One of them was elderly, and the others denied having been to Aberystwyth or knowing a Mark Bennett."

"Well, according to Bennett, Yates is nervous about anyone knowing his sexuality. So, he may hide his identity. I suspect, Stephen Yates is not his real name. Bennett claims that he met Yates on Grindr. I suggest you look him up on there and compare any profile photos with stills from the railway CCTV footage. I think if we are to find him, that is the way to go."

"We'll get on with it now." Sarah smiled. "It'll keep us out of mischief."

"Good." Yvonne sighed. "Listen, I will go home tonight. I'll be back early tomorrow morning. If anything happens, and you need me, call me on my home landline. But don't work too late, okay? I worked late last night and I am feeling it today. "

"We won't."

Their dedication to their job impressed her. They looked the part, too. Always neatly turned out and eager to learn. Their youthful idealism and optimism kept them going through the shear drudgery that was trawling through names and numbers. They still smiled — to her, at least.

Her mobile rang.

It was DCI Llewelyn. "Yvonne, how is it going down there?"

"Slowly, sir. Too slowly, for my liking. We have several suspects, but none that really jump out at me. I worry that we have a travelling killer. I've been scanning the papers, in case he's attacked elsewhere, but so far he has only struck in Aberystwyth. I'm wondering if he commutes here, either for work or just for his kills."

"Want me to come down?"

"Can you spare the time?"

"For a day or so, yes. I know I am only a phone call away, but it must be hard for you on your own up there. Have you heard from DCI Morgan?" Llewelyn asked, referring to the DCI in Cardigan, further down the Welsh coast, technically in charge of the Aberystwyth team.

"Only to find out if we've made progress. I think he

expects you to direct our operations because you are my line manager."

"Does he? I guess that is the downside to detectives crossing boundaries. No problem, I will spend the day with you tomorrow and take some weight off, okay? You sound tired. It'll do you good to have extra support."

"Thank you, sir. I appreciate it."

"Great. See you tomorrow."

## 18

## DISCLOSURE

That evening, Yvonne drove the hour-long commute home.

Tasha met her at the door, giving her a long hug. "I've missed you."

The DI closed her eyes, relishing the contact. "I've missed you, too."

"I've got a fire going." Tasha took Yvonne's coat. "And dinner is in the oven. Shepherd's pie."

"You're amazing." Yvonne grinned. "How did I live without you?"

The psychologist's food tasted as good as the aroma had promised. Yvonne held her stomach. "That's it. I am stuffed. I couldn't eat another thing."

"I've made egg custard." Tasha grimaced.

"Oh, how could you?" Yvonne laughed. "That is my favourite desert and I won't even manage one mouthful."

"Don't worry about it. It'll keep. I'll leave it in the fridge and you can have some for supper, or with your breakfast. How's that?"

"Sounds like a plan. How was your day?" Yvonne took Tasha's hand and led her to the lounge, throwing a blanket and cushions on the rug in front of the fire.

"It was quiet. I popped into town for a few provisions and then settled to preparing one of two profiles I had to do for Thames Valley Police."

"Thames Valley?" Yvonne raised an eyebrow. "Not the Met, this time?"

"No. I produce profiles for other forces, yours included, but I'm utilised more by the London Met."

"Did you finish it?"

"Pretty much. I need to go over it tomorrow before sending to them. Some subtle refining may be needed, but then it's off."

"Well done, you. Sounds like a productive day."

"What about yourself?"

"Me? Oh, my case is going absolutely nowhere. I am going around in circles, achieving little to nothing. Or, at least, that is how it feels."

"Well, we have a fire, and cushions, and time. Why don't you tell me where you are at? I have some idea of the case, after visiting the murder scenes with you."

Once settled, Yvonne related the gist of what her team knew so far.

Tasha listened intently, an arm around the DI as the latter related events.

When finished, Yvonne left for the kitchen to make two mugs of hot chocolate, leaving Tasha to think over what she'd said.

On her return, the psychologist gratefully accepted her chocolate. "How did Dewi get on when he looked at the registered sex offenders?"

"He's still going through the list." Yvonne sighed. "So far, he has found no links with these attacks. Most have cast iron alibis. The rest are paedophiles interested in far younger victims."

Tasha grimaced.

"We are trying to trace one or two people, perhaps one of them will help crack the case open." Yvonne shrugged. "I just know it won't be long before this killer takes another life. His cooling-off period is weeks, not months."

"Would you like me to prepare a profile?"

"Could you spare the time?"

"For you? Absolutely, I can."

Yvonne smiled. "Well, only if you're sure. The DCI will be there to support us, tomorrow. I can ask him about you going onto the payroll, if you are working with us."

"Whatever, you don't have to. I'd do it for you, anyway."

"I know. I don't want to take advantage."

"You won't. You don't."

Yvonne stared into the flames, her brow furrowed.

"Is something else bothering you?" Tasha tilted her head to better see Yvonne's eyes.

"I feel guilty that I am not out on the streets of Aberystwyth looking for him. What if he chooses tonight to strike again?"

"You're entitled to rest, Yvonne. You need it. You'll be no good to your team or to those girls if you end up exhausted. Tomorrow you can fight again, with DCI Superman Llewelyn at the helm."

Yvonne laughed. "Don't, you just gave me an image of him in a cape, and tight red undies over his trousers. It wasn't a good look."

"Eeew." Tasha laughed. "Did you have to?"

Yvonne felt better already. Time spent with Tasha was very, very precious.

∽

THE FOLLOWING MORNING, DCI Llewelyn arrived in Aberystwyth barely five minutes after Yvonne.

She gave him a quarter of an hour to settle in before going to see him.

"Come in."

"Are you okay?" she asked, on seeing him standing at the desk, both hands in his hair.

"Yes, yes, I'm fine. I'm just trying to find my way around. I was about to come and see you, actually. What's the matter?"

"You're looking unusually casual, sir." She was eyeing his blue jeans and grey sweater.

He looked down at his attire and grinned. "I'm anonymous here. I can get away with it. Besides, the paparazzi left me alone. I don't look important enough, obviously."

"So, it's a cunning disguise? Very good."

"Would you like me to look at what you've got already?"

"That would be great, sir. I'll fetch the paperwork and photographs for you to examine at your leisure. I need to talk to you, though."

"Is now okay? You can brief me and then I'll look at your case notes."

"Now is good." She nodded.

"Fire away."

"I was wondering if you would consider putting Tasha on the payroll again for this investigation. She will prepare a profile for us and she is prepared to travel here to do it. I think it a little unfair to expect her to go to that trouble and expense without some compensation."

"This is a difficult and increasingly high-profile inquiry, Yvonne. I think we can put a perfectly good case to the crime commissioner. I don't see it being any great difficulty. Under the circumstances, I believe he will agree to it."

"That's great." She smiled, but her body tensed. "There's something you ought to know before you approach the commissioner." She pulled a face, as though constipated.

"Yes? What is it? What's wrong?"

"It's myself and Tasha. We're partners. She's living with me. We're an item."

He did a double-take. "You're... You're what?"

"A couple."

"Right. Right. Erm, I see."

"It's okay, sir, you can have a minute to get your head around it, if you like?"

"No, it's fine. I... How long?"

"Several months."

"And you didn't tell me?"

"I was getting around to it."

"Congratulations," he said, his eyes scanning her face. "Well, I guess now I know why you and I didn't happen."

This was awkward. She cleared her throat. "It wasn't because of Tasha."

"Seriously, I'm happy for you. I'm happy for you both. I won't say I'm not surprised. I didn't exactly see it coming, but I am genuinely pleased for you."

"Are you still willing to allow her on the team for this case?"

"I see no reason not to. It's a consultancy role, so I don't see a conflict. If, however, the relationship disrupts your work, it shall force me to reconsider."

"Thank you, sir. It won't interfere with our work. We're both professionals."

"Good. Now, if you bring me the case notes, I'll go through it all and see if I can be of any help."

"Thank you."

She let out a sigh of relief as she walked the corridor to fetch her files. She hadn't expected it to be so easy. If only the case was that easy.

## 19

## BURIED IN THE SAND

Dewi grabbed her after she dropped the notes with the DCI. "The pathologist has been on the phone. Apparently they re-tested samples swabbed from Kathy Swales and found trace amounts of foreign DNA. He said they will carry out PCR, today and tomorrow, to amplify the DNA and hope to have a profile for us soon after that."

"Wow, that's fantastic news. Where did the DNA come from?"

"They were samples taken from her reproductive tract, ma'am. They retested samples with a new kit that provides an even greater sensitivity. Enzyme tests confirmed trace amounts of seminal fluid. They warned there's a high chance of contamination because of the tiny amounts involved, but they are still hopeful of giving us a profile we can use."

"Excellent. That is excellent, Dewi. It may not be from the murderer, especially if he wore a condom, but condoms sometimes burst or have holes in them and we could be lucky."

"I thought you'd be excited." Dewi grinned. "I'll make us a brew to celebrate."

∼

Yvonne stared out of the window, across the fields, as the light faded and dusk encroached. "I'm going out," she called to Dewi, grabbing her coat and leaving the office without looking back.

Firing up the engine of her car, she set off, face determined, lips in a tight line.

She parked in the churchyard, just behind the beautifully gothic edifice that was the Old College, and walked down to the rocky beach via the promenade. She didn't know what she looking for, only that she had an urge to look over the place where they had found Kathy Swales' body.

The killer had spent a significant time with Kathy. Not only had he persuaded her to walk with him along the promenade and down to the beach, he had had more time with her body. The time and place made it unlikely anyone would see him. He could adulterate and stage her at his leisure.

She crouched near to where the girl had sat staring out to sea, running her eyes over the stones, wondering exactly where the attack had started.

A dog bark had her jumping up, heart pounding, she put a hand to her chest.

"Benji," a voice called. It was Keith Griffiths in an anorak.

Her heart continued to thump. "You gave me a fright," she said, taking a step backward.

"What are you doing?" he asked, stopping in his tracks.

"I'm thinking. What are you doing?"

"Er, walking my dog?"

Benji ran to her legs, sniffing around her ankles. He gave several more barks before sniffing a trail to a spot between the edge of the stone and the water, barking repeatedly at the sand before digging at it in a frenzy.

"Benji," Griffiths shouted.

The dog took no notice, grabbing something in his mouth and tugging at it, ripping it out of the wet sand.

Yvonne and Keith Griffiths began running the same time, the DI pulling an evidence bag from her pocket.

Luckily, she was closer to Benji than Griffiths was. She grabbed at what she thought was a rag in the dog's mouth, using the open evidence bag. The dog let go just before Keith Griffiths joined her.

She sealed the bag.

"What was that?" Griffiths asked.

Yvonne held the bag up, examining it in the little light there was left. "Looks like gloves." She turned to Griffiths. "Wait, you don't think they're the gloves you lost, do you?"

"I doubt it." He held out his hand. "Can I see?"

There was something menacing about his dark outline against the backdrop of the sea.

She swallowed hard, shaking her head, wishing she wasn't so alone. "No." She faked confidence. "Because of the location we found them, I'll take them in for testing. When we've finished with them, if they are yours, you can come and claim them."

She couldn't see his expression but felt he was scowling at her.

"Enjoy your walk," she called, as she turned to head back up the rocks and the steps to the pavement above, almost tripping in her haste to get out of there.

## 20

## WHO IS LYING?

She had barely dealt with submitting the gloves for testing, when Sarah and Ifan caught up with her.

Eyes shining, and speaking fast, Ifan hit her with it. "We've found Stephen Yates, ma'am. Real name Samuel Oakley. We've spoken with him on the phone and he states that he hasn't slept with Bennett. He said Bennett was messing him about and he doubts that Bennett is even gay."

"Have you got an address for Oakley?"

"Better than that, ma'am. He has agreed to come and see us, tomorrow, if we reimburse his travel fare. He'll be coming in by train."

"Great. Make sure everything is ready for him and I agree to paying his travel expenses. I'll speak with the DCI to find out if he can be here again tomorrow. If Samuel Oakley checks out, and is believable, we'll be pulling Bennett in for questioning and possibly placing him under arrest."

"Yes, ma'am."

DCI LLEWELLYN HAD AGREED to be in Aberystwyth again the following day and accompanied Yvonne for the interview with Samuel Oakley AKA Stephen Yates.

The DI tapped her pen on the desk, reading through the questions she planned to ask Samuel. He ought to have been there already, but an incident on the line had delayed his train.

DCI Llewelyn joined her. "Are we ready?" he asked, dressed in full uniform in contrast to his casual look, the day before.

"I am, but Oakley hasn't arrived, yet."

"He has. Ifan is making him a coffee as we speak."

"He's here?" She pulled a face. "Why am I the last to know?"

DCI Llewelyn grinned. "You were miles away, or you'd have noticed the sudden activity."

Sarah met them in the corridor. "Oakley is in interview room one. He was hungry, so we gave him a lunch pack. Hope that's okay?"

Yvonne nodded. "That's fine, he can eat it while we settle in. We could be in there a while. What's your impression of him?"

"He seems genuine, ma'am. A little timid, maybe. He looks younger than his age."

"All right, thanks."

As they joined him across the table, Samuel Oakley ate the sandwiches as though he hadn't had food in a week. He looked it too, with his slight frame, gaunt face and ashen pallor. His fair hair, flopping around his face, looked like it had been cut by a mate after a few pints too many. Though his clothes looked fairly clean, there was a faint whiff about him. The smell of the street.

"Hi Sam. Is it Sam? Or Samuel?" Yvonne began.

"Sam's fine," he said, brushing crumbs from his thighs.

"I understand you live in Shrewsbury?"

"Yeah, at the moment. I was living at my mum and dad's house, but I moved out two months ago. I've been sofa-surfing since then."

"Why did you move away from your parents' home if you didn't have an address to go to?"

"Sick of the arguments. They don't understand me and they don't like my friends."

"Can I ask why they don't like your friends?"

He shrugged. "They just don't like their lifestyle."

"And what is their lifestyle?"

He didn't answer.

"Have you got a support worker? Anyone to help you?"

Sam shook his head.

"We can't refer you in for support, unfortunately, as it is out of our area, but we could put you in touch with colleagues in West Mercia who could. If you would like the help?"

He shrugged.

"Tell me about Mark Bennett. How did you two meet?"

"Grindr. I've been using it for a while. As you've probably worked out, I'm gay. I'm not out, though. Some of my friends are. That's why my parents don't like me hanging around with them. My parents are old-fashioned."

"Did you approach Mark on Grindr? Or did he approach you?"

"He approached me."

"Okay. Then what happened?"

"We agreed to meet up a few times."

"DC Hughes tells me you don't think Mark Bennett is gay. Why is that?"

Sam grunted, leaning back in his chair, putting his

hands in the pockets of his jeans. "Well, I've stayed with him three times altogether, and we haven't been physical."

"What happens when you visit him?" Yvonne's eyes narrowed.

"Well, he meets me at the station and we go for food, or order a takeaway. We have slept in the same bed, but he never tries to touch me."

"Has he offered you money?"

"I don't charge." Sam glared at her. "What do you take me for?"

"I wasn't implying that you did, I'm just trying to work out what Mark Bennett was looking for."

"Company, I guess. He can be gruff. Not what I expected, considering he told me he wants to transition."

"So, he told you he wants to be a woman?"

"Yes, he said that. I don't get that vibe from him, though."

"Do you think he's not serious about it?"

"I expected him to behave more like a female than he did."

"Do you think he was lying to you?"

"I didn't believe his story, so yes."

"I see. Can I take you back to the night of Monday the third of December? You stayed with Mark. Is that correct?"

"Yes. He met me off the train the evening before."

"So, Sunday the second of December?"

"Yes. We got a takeaway and watched TV with a few beers. We slept together, but he fell asleep virtually straight away. We did a bit of shopping the following day, had lunch out, and then he had to go to an evening shift at the hospital."

"He went to work?"

"Yes. He let me stay at the flat all night, while he was gone. He knew I was getting the six o'clock train the following morning, and he said he would meet me there and see me off."

"So, he didn't go with you to the station?"

"No, he met me there."

"You're sure of that?"

Sam frowned. "Yes, of course I'm sure. I wouldn't forget that, would I?"

"Did he tell you whether he had come straight from the hospital?"

"No. He didn't say."

"Thank you, Sam. If we need to speak with you again, how do we reach you?"

"I have a mobile. I gave the number to the other officer."

"DCs Hughes and Evans?"

"Yes."

"Good, we'll call you if we need to ask you anything further."

"Can I have the train fare back?" He looked at her, wide-eyed.

"We'll do better than that. You can have the rail fare and lunch money."

Sam grinned. "Thanks."

∾

AS THEY WALKED BACK to the main office, Llewelyn paused. "Do you have enough to arrest Bennett?" he asked Yvonne.

"Possibly. It looks like he lied to us about his whereabouts the morning Amanda Hartnett was murdered, his colleague reported suspicious absences, he had female clothing with him, and Sam thinks that Mark is not telling the truth about transitioning. We have a case building. I don't want to arrest him yet, however, I think I would like to talk to the consultant Mark told me about. After all, if he is having appointments for gender transition, Sam's suspicions could be wrong."

"He still lied about his whereabouts."

She nodded. "He did. You're right. We'll interview him and see what he has to say. I can follow up by talking to his physician, later."

Llewelyn nodded. "Of your suspects, so far, Bennett is one of two that stand out for me."

"Who is the other one?" she asked. "Let me guess, Keith Griffiths?"

Llewelyn shook his head. "I would say John Lloyd."

"I see. I got a different impression from meeting him. Right, sir, I had better get on with it. Got a man to bring in."

∾

Mark Bennett came in the same afternoon. He waited in the interview room while Yvonne caught up with Dewi.

"Keith Griffiths has agreed to come in for a DNA swab." Dewi took his jacket off and placed it on the back of his chair. "He knows we will compare it to any found on the gloves and stated to me this morning that he thinks the gloves might be his."

"Interesting." Yvonne pursed her lips. "Okay. Don't tell him we have a DNA profile taken from Kathy Swales' body, in case he retracts his permission. Have they gotten back to us about the gloves?"

"We should have a DNA profile from them tomorrow, ma'am."

"All right, good work, Dewi. Keep me informed."

"Will do."

BENNETT HAD his arms folded across his chest, leaning back in the chair, a terse look on his face.

Yvonne took a deep breath. "Sorry to keep you, Mark. We just need a couple minutes more, while we wait for my DCI to join us."

"I'm due in work in an hour," he said, looking at his watch. "

"We'll do our best to finish before then, but that will depend in part upon you."

"What do you mean?"

DCI Llewelyn knocked and walked in.

Yvonne introduced herself and the others for the recording and began. "Mark, we have asked you back in, as we have spoken to Stephen Yates and his version of events does not tally with yours."

"What?" Mark frowned. "What did he say?"

"Well, we asked him about his stay on Monday the third of December, the night before Amanda Hartnett's murder, and he states he is not your partner. He said you two were not physical as you showed no interest in being physical with him. And that you only came off shift at the hospital in time to meet him at the station, to see him off."

"He's lying." Mark spat.

"About which bit?"

"All of it. He said we were dating and the only reason we haven't been physical, so far, is that he wanted payment and I refused."

"He told me he has never sought payment."

"Well, like I said, he's lying. That guy wouldn't know the truth if it smacked him in the face. You know his real name isn't Stephen Yates, don't you?"

Yvonne rubbed her chin. "Do you know his real name?"

"Sam. I don't know his surname, but I was chatting to someone else on Grindr and they said his name is Sam. So, who is this guy, really?"

"It's not unusual for some people to have a pseudonym online. Some feel it safer to hide behind another name until they get to know who they are talking to."

"Are you making excuses for him?"

"I'm trying to see things from both sides."

"Yeah, well, he wanted me to pay him and I refused."

"How far along the path are you regarding your gender transition, Mark?"

"I should start treatment in the next few weeks."

"How many appointments have you had?"

"A few. Look, why does that matter?"

"Stephen Yates said that you met him at the station to see him off. Is that right?"

"No. Like I told you, I left my shift fifteen minutes early to meet him at home. We walked to the station together."

"That's not what he tells us. He also stated that you two had only met a few times, not every two weeks as you told me."

"Well, it was two weeks in between each meeting."

"He doesn't consider himself to be your boyfriend."

"Where is this going?"

"I'll be frank with you, Mark. I think you gave me a cover story that was only half the truth. I think you are hiding something and lying about your whereabouts. That could be because you murdered Amanda Hartnett on the seafront that morning and are desperate to cover up. I am also wondering whether you invited Stephen Yates down so that it would provide you with a cover story."

"That's ridiculous."

"Is it?"

"I didn't murder anyone. And I am telling the truth. Stephen Yates, or Sam, or whatever the hell they call him, asked me for money for sex and I met him at my flat before walking him to the station. That's it. Can I go, now? Or do I need to have a solicitor?"

Yvonne looked at the DCI, who nodded.

"You can go, for now. But don't leave the area. I will need to speak with you, again."

∽

LLEWELYN MADE them both coffee after the interview.

Yvonne had her hands in her hair. "Either Sam Oakley or Mark Bennett is lying, but which is it? Sam hides his identity and his sexuality, and could, in theory, be lying about wanting payment for sex. Bennett acts suspiciously in front of work colleagues and may be lying about his whereabouts on the morning of Amanda Hartnett's death. I'll ask Sarah and Ifan to pay a visit to Bennett's neighbours, see if they can shed light on whether they saw those two leaving together that morning. Although, at half-past-five, there may have been no one to witness them leaving the flat."

Llewelyn handed her a coffee. "Talk to Bennett's consultant. Find out what he thinks about Bennett's real intentions as regards transitioning gender. I agree, it's difficult, but you'll get to the bottom of it. Do you have Bennett's shift pattern? If not, get a copy. Monitor where he should be and when. If needs be, we'll get a tail on him."

"Yes, of course."

## 21

## DNA

The following morning, Dewi waited patiently for an email from pathology, to say whether they had a clear profile for the DNA from Kathy Swales and, separately, whether they had got anything from the gloves. He couldn't wait to tell Yvonne, when the confirmation came through that not only did they successfully produce a profile from the Kathy Swales sample, but that it matched with the one obtained from the gloves.

He found the DI working at the whiteboard, cross-referencing what they knew with what they needed to establish.

"Ma'am, DNA isolated from the leather gloves you found on the beach matches with the profile they got from Kathy Swales' body." He stopped to catch his breath. "Whoever buried those gloves, could be our man."

"Get on the phone and find out when we might have Keith Griffiths' DNA profile. We need to know for sure whether he was the owner of the gloves."

"Right."

"If the profiles match, I'll ask the DCI to sanction an arrest on suspicion."

"Yes, ma'am."

⁓

THERE HAD BEEN an issue with the first swab taken from Griffiths.

Frustratingly, Yvonne had to ask him in again. He agreed after complaining about the time it was taking from his work.

Yvonne met him in reception, and led him through for interview. "Can we swab your mouth for a further DNA test?" she asked, placing a pair of latex gloves and a testing kit on the desk.

"Yes. I can save you the trouble, though."

"What do you mean?" She tilted her head, eyes half-lidded.

"I think the gloves you found are mine."

"I know you do." She snapped on her latex ones. "I would still like to swab you, if that is okay?"

"Fine." He held his mouth open.

Yvonne rubbed the cotton tip around the inside of his cheek, ejecting it into the sterile fluid in the container which she then sealed. "We'll get this off to the lab and we'll know if the gloves are yours."

"They are mine. That was the place I was walking when I lost them."

"Why were you on that part of the beach?"

"I..." His voice trailed away, and he turned his head as though hiding something from her.

"Were you walking there because that is where Kathy Swales was murdered?"

"What? No." His words didn't jibe with the emotions in his eyes.

"You were, weren't you? You were returning to the place of her murder. I'll bet you walked that stretch every day with Benji. Convenient alibi, having a dog. Remorse, was it?"

"You don't know what you are talking about." His face reddened, the muscles tensing in anger.

She took hold of his arm. "Keith Griffiths, I am arresting you on suspicion of the murder of Kathy Swales. You do not have to say anything, but it may harm your defence if you do not mention, when questioned, something which you later rely on in court. Anything you do say may be given in evidence. Do you understand?"

"I didn't murder her."

"I will record that reply. I suggest you wait for your solicitor."

## 22

## PUZZLE PIECES

That afternoon, Tasha joined them at the station. Yvonne and the team awaited the outcome of Keith Griffiths' second DNA swab as the lecturer chilled in the cells pending formal interview.

The DI greeted Tasha in reception, her eyes lighting up. "Tasha, welcome to Aberystwyth police station." She grinned. "Come on, we're upstairs."

"Wow." Tasha attempted to take it all in as they walked. "This is a far cry from the old Victorian place," she said, referring to the former station on the seafront.

"It is." Yvonne smiled. To her mind, the facade of the modern build at Boulevard Saint Brieuc was a cross between a prison and a barn conversion — with a round tower stuck on the corner for good measure. It was unarguably a better workplace, more fit-for-purpose than the old station, but it lacked a certain character, she felt.

"We're upstairs in the incident room. We're going through exhibits and CCTV, taking stock of what we have. Anything you need, just ask."

"I will, thanks."

Yvonne paused, turning to her companion. "Thank you for coming in to help us. I really appreciate it. I know you would have helped me, anyway, but the good news is, you are officially on the payroll."

Tasha laughed. "This day just keeps getting better."

"You have the DCI to thank for that."

"And a certain DI that I have a particular interest in."

Yvonne grinned. "Behave, we're at work and this is a serious investigation. I've been tearing my hair out, I need you focussed. We need your help more than ever, Tasha."

"No problem, I'm good."

The DI introduced Tasha to Ifan and Sarah who gave her all she needed to produce the offender profile.

The psychologist found herself a quiet corner and got to work immediately.

∾

DEWI BENT OVER, catching his breath. "Ma'am, we have the results of the DNA analysis from Keith Griffiths. Sorry, I've just run up the stairs."

Yvonne tossed her notes down onto the desk. "Well, come on, Dewi. Don't keep me in suspense."

He straightened up. "The DNA from the gloves and from Kathy Swales are a match with Keith Griffiths." His eyes shone with excitement. "We may have our murderer."

"A match?" Yvonne grinned and pumped the air with her fist. "Yes. He knew they were his. He knew we would find out. That man has some explaining to do."

"I can't wait to see how he explains what they were doing buried there," Dewi agreed.

"Make sure he has his solicitor present." Yvonne straightened her clothes. "I want to interview him as soon as possible. Can you ensure we have the data from the comparisons, so I can show them to him?"

"Absolutely." Dewi nodded. "I'll see that everything you need is to hand. Is the DCI going to be here for it?"

"I don't know, Dewi. I may have Tasha in the interview with me. Thank you for this. Good work."

## 23

## CONUNDRUM

Keith Griffiths finished the conference with his solicitor as Yvonne and Tasha entered the room and took their seats opposite.

Yvonne introduced them all for the recording and reminded Griffiths he was under caution.

She placed documents on the table between them, purposely taking her time with each, to emphasise their significance.

Griffiths opened the top button of his shirt and loosened his tie, clearing his throat.

"Doctor Griffiths, I have placed in front of you three DNA profiles, we received from forensics this morning. What do you notice about them?"

He examined each of the traces and, though the room was a cool twenty degrees centigrade, a perceptible layer of sweat developed on his upper lip. "They all look the same." He lifted his eyes to hers, his pupils huge.

"You should tell my client what he is looking at." Griffiths' broad-shouldered solicitor pushed his glasses up his nose.

"Of course." Yvonne nodded, flicking Tasha a quick glance. "What we have are the DNA traces from your cheek swab, your leather gloves, and from the reproductive tract of the murder victim Kathy Swales. As you can see, the profiles match exactly. What do you have to say about that?"

Griffiths looked at his solicitor. He appeared lost, floundering, his eyes wide, his mouth open. Searching for the right words. Any words.

"Can I have a moment with my client?" Griffiths' solicitor requested.

Yvonne nodded. "Of course."

She gave Tasha a nod and the two of them rose from their seats and left the room.

"Did you see the look on his face?" Yvonne asked Tasha, as they waited in the corridor.

Tasha rubbed her chin. "That floored him. He would have known his DNA would match with the gloves as he knew they were his. Evidently, what shocked him was his DNA being found inside Kathy. He's scared about that, I think that's obvious."

"He knows we've got him." Yvonne leaned back against the wall, pursing her lips. "Why would he be surprised about his DNA being found in Kathy? Surely, he would have expected it?"

"Unless he thought he'd a good enough job, leaving her in water, and that the traces would have been washed away or destroyed?"

"Yes, he probably believed he'd done enough to destroy the evidence. He looks terrified. Good." The DI straightened up when Keith Griffiths' solicitor opened the door to let them know they could return.

"I've spoken with my client, and he has an explanation

for his DNA being present in the murder victim." He nodded to Griffiths.

Griffiths cleared his throat. "I had sex with Kathy Swales two days before her murder."

Yvonne leaned forward, her elbows on the desk. "Wait, I'm not clear, are you saying you had consensual sex with her? Two days before her murder?"

"Yes, I am."

"Why are you telling me this now? When I interviewed you previously, you denied any sexual impropriety with Kathy, stating you had only ever talked to her whilst smoking on the campus."

"I know." He shook his head, staring at the table and sighing.

"And now, you want me to believe the sex you had with Kathy was consensual?"

"It was." He looked up, his eyes pleading. "We had been flirting for some time. I admit, it was mostly me to start with but, latterly, she had taken to flirting back. I would even say she took over as the lead instigator. Then, she came to me one day, crying. She was struggling with her work and needed a shoulder. I provided that shoulder and, well, one thing led to another."

"So, why didn't you tell me this before?" Yvonne frowned, shaking her head.

"I have a wife. She would never forgive me for this. I would lose her. Things got out of hand."

"You have a reputation for flouting boundaries with female students, Doctor Griffiths. Did you ever consider your wife's feelings? Except, now, you tell me you have concerns and you're worried about losing her? Kathy Swales lost her life. I think that is the greater loss, would you not agree, Doctor Griffiths? Where were your pangs of conscience when you were actively taking advantage of that vulnerable young woman?"

"I wouldn't have said she was vulnerable-"

"No? She was distressed, crying, and she came to you for reassurance. Do you not think, in that moment, she was extremely vulnerable? You said yourself, she needed a shoulder, and you were more than happy to provide it. You took advantage. I view that as unacceptable."

Griffiths sighed, his whole body shuddering. "I hadn't planned to take advantage of her. I thought we could have a little fun. She may have been young, but she was still an adult and able to decide for herself."

"That's called Justification." Yvonne folded her arms. "And, I think it rather convenient that you lay this story on me now. Now, when we have enough evidence here to prosecute you for her murder."

"I didn't murder Kathy. I would never... could never have done that. Believe it or not, I cared about that girl. I cared about her very much. You can't have an affair with someone without developing feelings." Griffiths' face contorted as though he was in pain.

"Did she threaten to expose you?"

"What?"

"Did you kill two more girls to cover up the crime? Make it look like a serial killer was at work?"

"Now, hang on-" Griffiths' solicitor raised a hand.

"Or was Kathy, and the others used to sate your diabolical urges because you are a psychopath, and that is how you get off?"

"I told you, I didn't kill her and I had nothing whatsoever to do with those other girls. Not a flirtation, not an affair, and definitely not murder."

Griffiths' solicitor again intervened. "I would like more time alone with my client."

Yvonne rose from her seat. "Interview suspended, one-fifteen pm"

∼

THE FOLLOWING DAY, Yvonne found herself in the magistrates' court fighting for Keith Griffiths to stay on remand.

Her eyes followed the curves and folds of the oversized coat of arms on the wall above the three magistrates, as they sat on the bench, talking amongst themselves. In front of her was Keith Griffiths' defence solicitor alongside the CPS representative. The latter fighting her corner. The two solicitors discussed a football match they had seen on the television the night before, debating the strengths and weaknesses of the two sides.

The DI pursed her lips. She knew solicitors spent a great deal of time in court together and needed to be civil. It just didn't seem right that they should laugh and joke with each other in the recesses when so much was at stake. She knew she was being unreasonable, but she felt like physically parting them.

She didn't.

The CPS representative, Gareth Owen, turned around to face her. "Griffiths has corroboration for what he argues was the consensual sex he had with the victim two days before the murder. He has a witness who states they saw Kathy Swales go up to Griffiths and ask him to go with her to her room."

Yvonne frowned. "Who?"

"Another student apparently. A letter has been produced for the court, written by the student. The magistrates are examining it, now. If the case goes to trial, the witness will be cross-examined but, as for this bail hearing, that letter will probably have him released."

"What?" Yvonne grimaced. "Please be joking. They should not let Keith Griffiths out on bail. Not when he is a serious suspect for those horrific murders?"

Owen shrugged. "I'll make that case for you, of course, but don't get your hopes up, Yvonne. I am concerned you may no longer have enough to bring this to trial. Keith Griffiths will probably walk out of her today, pending the pre-trial hearing, if we get that far."

And walk, Keith Griffiths did.

Yvonne felt utterly dejected. Shoulders hunched, her gut knotted and nauseous, she met Tasha outside for what should have been a triumphant lunch. Instead, the DI decided she would have only coffee while she pondered where this left her and her case.

Tasha placed a hand on her shoulder as they walked away from the court. "Look, Griffiths isn't your only suspect. We'll take stock and look over what we have. From what you've said, Mark Bennett still has a lot of explaining to do. Take a step back and think about the overall case. Don't get caught up in this minor setback. You'll figure it out. And you can always have Griffiths watched in the meantime."

Yvonne leaned her head on Tasha's shoulder. "You're right. I know you're right, Tasha. I can always rely on you to talk some sense into me. I'll be fine in an hour or two. Let's go get you some lunch."

## 24

## MORE QUESTIONS THAN ANSWERS

Tasha waited for the hubbub to die down, reading through her presentation one last time, making sure it lay out all the points.

Once she had everyone's attention, she flicked to the first slide in Power Point as the noise abated.

She had their respect. She could see it in the eager faces, rolled-up sleeves, pen's behind ears, and hands on hips. Their silence underlined it.

She switched on her laser pointer. "I believe the person you are looking for is a male, aged between thirty and fifty years of age. He's strong and fit and may have a job that involves physicality. If not, he'll likely be a regular at the gym, or some other form of fitness, perhaps a martial art?"

She continued. "This is someone who inspires trust in those he is about to victimise. One particular victim trusted him so much, he could persuade her to accompany him along the promenade in the early hours of the morning. I suspect he has a non-threatening manner and friendly demeanour. He may be in a caring profession or have a nurturing role. It is possible he uses a disguise, or prop, to aid in his credibility, giving him the maximum time and ability to take his victim unawares. Perhaps he persuades them to go with him to look for something. A lost dog or a wallet, for instance."

She flicked forward two slides. "We have reason to suspect him of being a necrophile. If this is the case, he would be in the category of genuine necrophile, because he acts out his fantasy in real life. He is also a homicidal necrophile, meaning, he kills to fulfil his desires of having sex with a corpse. This man will have encountered death at an early age, possibly of someone who had been abusing him, but who had offered him the only physical closeness he had ever known. He may have had cold or distant parents and craved affection, even that of an abuser. If you are cross-referencing sex-offender records, a history of that sort would put the subject at a higher likelihood of committing these offences than someone who did not have this type of history. If he is a necrophile, he is forensically aware and uses condoms to ensure he doesn't leave his DNA. He has, however, left copious fibres on his victims despite being forensically aware. This lends support to the idea that he purchases clothing purposely for these attacks, then discards it afterwards, gaining more prior to the next attack."

She flicked to the final slide, summarising what she had just outlined. "Questions?"

"When you say a caring or nurturing profession, are you thinking of nurses and carers?" Ifan asked, pen at the ready.

"They would be examples of what I am talking about. This is a university town so it could also be tutors or mentors. Anyone, with a role in welfare, really."

. . .

Following Tasha's presentation, Yvonne caught up with Dewi. "Can you look into Keith Griffiths' background? Find out what his childhood was like? I realise it won't be easy, but any information you can dig up around his relationships could prove useful."

"Sure." Dewi nodded. "What are you going to do?" He eyed her, as she put on her jacket.

"I have a man to see."

"Oh, yeah? Is there something you're not telling me?" He grinned.

Yvonne laughed. "Nothing that exciting, I'm afraid. I'm off for a chat with Mark Bennett's consultant. I think the porter still has a lot of questions to answer and I need to know what he is up to."

"Right, I'd better get on, myself." Dewi wiped a hand across his forehead in dramatic fashion. "My DI is a slave driver, I'll get into trouble." He winked at her.

"If I was a slave driver, Dewi Hughes, you'd know about it. I drive myself far harder than I ever drive you. However, that could change..."

He gave her a mock salute. "On it, like a car bonnet, ma'am."

~

Doctor Hassall cut an imposing figure in his unblemished white coat. With his stethoscope around his neck and hands in his trouser pockets, she could see how his neatly trimmed beard, observant gaze, and self-possession would inspire confidence in those he advised and treated. Her own impression was of a highly competent surgeon. She also suspected he was not the type to suffer fools gladly.

As the light faded, and the streetlights came on, he

seated himself at the computer to open Mark Bennett's file and remind himself of the important details.

Yvonne waited patiently for his verdict, her eyes travelling the room to the treatment bed, textbooks, medical equipment, desk, and back to Hassall.

His deep voice vibrated through her thoughts. "Well, Inspector Giles, Mark Bennett has yet to attend any of our offered appointments."

"He has attended nothing at all?" Yvonne raised an eyebrow, shaking her head. "Why?"

Hassall sighed. "Your guess is as good as mine."

"Well, I wasn't expecting that."

"Neither were we. To be perfectly frank, I would question his desire to transition at all."

"Then why go to the trouble of approaching you? Has he got cold feet?"

"You'd have to ask him that."

"And he hasn't offered you an explanation for his absences?"

"None."

"Is that usual?"

"It happens." Hassall nodded. "Some people back off when it becomes a reality. But that is only rarely, and usually after they have attended at least one of the consultancy appointments. People usually have a fair idea of what they are committing to, or walking away from, before they attend for consultation. Google is their friend. They will probably also have been to support groups and talked to people who have themselves transitioned. Looking at his answers to the questionnaire they gave him when signing up, I don't believe Bennet has any real idea of what it involves."

"I see."

"I've the feeling he has messed us about from the beginning. I don't know why he would do that, but I find it frustrating. Waiting lists are long enough without this brand of thoughtless behaviour. I'm sure he'd be different if the bill for mine and others' time fell onto his doormat."

"Quite." Yvonne scratched her head. "Did he warn you that he would not attend?"

"Not that I know of. He may have informed reception but, if he did, the message never reached me."

"Right."

Hassall clicked his tongue, hands on hips. "I won't be offering him another appointment, Inspector. If he wants treatment, he must go further afield."

"I can't say I blame you." Yvonne rose to leave. "Doctor Hassall, thank you for your time. You have been very helpful."

"You're welcome. I'm glad I could help."

## 25

## PREY

As Yvonne left Hassall's office, the world had gone dark.

She checked her watch. Six o'clock. According to the rota Bennett had given her, he was due to start his shift at seven. If she ate straight away, she could be at the hospital to catch him while he was getting ready, before the shift began.

She grabbed her mobile and rang Tasha's number. If the psychologist hadn't eaten yet, they could grab something together.

When Tasha answered, she sounded like she was finishing a mouthful.

"Ah, you're already eating." Yvonne sighed. "Sorry, I'm too late."

"I grabbed a sandwich." The psychologist apologised. "I hadn't eaten since twelve-thirty, and I was starving. Dewi told me you were at the hospital interviewing a consultant, so I just assumed you wouldn't be free to meet."

"Yeah, it's no problem. I was just going to suggest the

Italian on North Parade. But, I tell you what, we'll go tomorrow if we get a chance."

"Sounds like a plan," Tasha agreed. "Are you staying in Aberystwyth, tonight?"

"I am. I have a room at a bed-and-breakfast in the harbour. You're welcome to join me, if you want to stay."

"I want to stay and so, yes, I'd like that. I have a feeling this case is hotting up and I don't want to leave you on your own. I know what you're like."

Yvonne laughed. "I don't know where you get these ideas from, Tasha. I'm off to Bronglais Hospital, shortly. I'll see you back at the room."

With that, the DI gave Tasha the details for the bed-and-breakfast, and ended the call, determined to find herself food from the local Spar. She now only had thirty minutes to be at Bronglais, ready to speak to Bennett.

∽

As she walked the seemingly endless hospital corridors, Yvonne pondered what Hassall had said. Why would anyone go to the trouble of setting up appointments for a life-changing intervention and not only not turn up, but not make a courtesy call to explain? She was still pondering this, when she heard a raised voice further along the corridor. The place she was heading.

She could see a tall, slender dark-haired man with a moustache gesticulating at a woman who was leaning away from him. She recognised his target as Fran Owen, Mark Bennett's closest colleague. She hastened her stride.

By the time she reached Fran, the angry man had gone. "Are you okay?" Yvonne asked her, tilting her head.

Fran had tears in her eyes. "Yes. Yes, I'm fine. Now you

can see why we call him The Fuehrer. He can be a nightmare. I wouldn't mind if it was my fault. "She shrugged.

"Some people enjoy throwing their weight around." Yvonne wanted to put a hand on Fran's shoulder. She didn't. "Don't let it affect you."

Fran shook her head. "I try not to." She held up her hands. They were shaking. "You see what it does?"

"I'm assuming the hospital has an anti-bullying policy?" Yvonne frowned. "Why have they not challenged him about his behaviour? Have you reported it?"

Fran shook her head. "He's the boss. I don't want any trouble. I just want to do my job and go home. I'm a fan of the easy life. Anyway, they are more interested in targets. He hits his targets."

Yvonne pursed her lips. "Well, from where I am standing, your job looks far from easy. Surely, he has line managers above him. Can't you speak to them?"

She shrugged.

Yvonne sighed. "I'm actually here to speak to Mark Bennett. Is he about?"

Fran shook her head. "That's partly what that was all about." She gestured towards where Paul Heston had disappeared.

"What do you mean?"

"Mark telephoned in earlier, explaining that he wouldn't be in and asking to rearrange his shift. Some sort of emergency, I think."

"I see. Did he say what?"

Fran shook her head. "I assume it is something to do with his mum but, to be honest, I have all but given up on him. I don't think he'll survive in the job much longer, the way he is going. Heston's mad as hell about him at the moment. He's left us short-staffed. I will work on my own until Heston can persuade another colleague to come in and cover. If he can reach anyone."

"I'm sorry to hear that, Fran." Yvonne felt genuinely sad for the woman. "And I was serious, don't take that kind of punishment from your line manager, and especially not for something which is not your fault. Talk to someone. A higher manager or a union rep. Anyone, who can help you fight back."

Fran nodded. "I will. I'll speak to my union rep. I hadn't thought of that, it might be a good place to start."

Yvonne smiled. "Good for you. Right, I will look for Mark at the care home. If he turns up here, would you be so good as to give him this card? Tell him Inspector Giles wants a word. Ask him to call me."

"Yes, I will, Inspector."

"Thank you."

As she walked back to her car, Yvonne blew on her hands. The temperature had dropped significantly. In the distance, a silvery mist curled in off the sea.

~

THE MUSIC THUMP, thumped, leaving Hannah hedonistically lost in it. She could see Shaunagh and Chloe attempting to converse above the music, shouting into each other's ears. It looked painful, and this song was one of her favourites. She was enjoying cutting shapes and didn't want to do anything but move. Besides, people always looked awkward when dancing and talking at the same, like they were nervous or something. She couldn't deny that the several shots she had knocked back were amplifying the feel-good factor, they included two Jaeger bombs. This was a good night. This was a brilliant night. She could lose herself in it.

Strobe lighting made everyone and everything jerky, further enhancing the alcohol-fuelled trance Hannah was experiencing. She tossed her head back, throwing her hands in the air in time to the pounding beat.

∽

*He watched her getting carried away with the music, oblivious to everyone around her. The girl had been drinking far faster than her friends. She should be careful. If she consumed any more alcohol, she'd lose her balance. Perhaps, that's why she held a hand up when one of her mates gestured towards the bar. Good. If she started falling over, it would be a taxi home. No chance she'd be walking. And he hoped she would walk. He willed her to walk.*

*In the meantime, he watched her slender body as she pulsed to the music. So animated, now. If he had his way, she'd be a lot less animated, later.*

## 26

## THE MIST MOVES IN

Pant Glas care home was quiet. The residents, having consumed their evening meal, had dispersed and were watching television in their rooms or settled in front of the communal set in the lounge.

Pam Williams signed Yvonne in.

"Thanks." Yvonne loosened her scarf. "I was hoping I would find Harriet Bennett's son Mark here."

Pam shook her head. "I'm sorry, Inspector. We haven't seen Mark for several days. His mum Harriet has fallen asleep in her room and I don't really want to disturb her."

"So, there has been no emergency this evening?"

"No, no emergency here. It's been quiet. Why?"

"I thought there might have been one, that's all." The DI didn't think it her place to say any more.

Pam rubbed her chin. "It's been this quiet since tea time. We've definitely not had anything kicking off."

"I see." Yvonne frowned. "Listen, if Mark comes here, could you call me?"

Pam accepted her card. "Yes, of course."

Yvonne saw herself out.

～

Hannah had had enough. She'd had more than enough alcohol and as much excitement as she could handle. She was tired, and had an urgent desire to be home in her pjs, with pizza and something on telly.

She looked around for Shaunagh and Chloe. They were on the dance floor, still fending off admirers. She waved to them but they didn't see her. Too many bodies in the way.

She almost lost her footing as she wandered to the door, checking in her pocket for her ticket to collect her belongings. At first, she couldn't find it, sighing with relief when she got it from the last place she looked for it. There were so many pockets in her jeans.

She hiccoughed and made her way to back of the tiny queue of people waiting for their stuff. She really ought to let her friends know she was going, but decided it would be easier to text them on her way home. Her mobile phone was in her bag.

～

*She had left her friends behind.*

*He could see her rifling through her bag, reassuring herself that all of its contents were still present, even though the receptacle had been safe in a ticketed closet for the last several hours.*

*She nearly lost her balance again, oblivious to him, the predator observing her every move. Perhaps, he ought to stand behind her. Be there to catch her when she fell. And he was sure she would fall. They always did.*

## 27

## REALISATION

Yvonne walked arm-in-arm with Tasha, alongside the harbour, on their way to the bed-and-breakfast. They could see the nearside boats enough to read their names but those further away disappeared in the enveloping mist.

"I hope he's not out tonight." Yvonne shuddered.

"Are you okay?" Tasha placed an arm around her shoulders.

The DI paused, turning to her. "What if the man Shaunagh observed following Alice Brierley was nothing to do with her murder? She said he spooked her, and she had bad vibes, but we know he could have been entirely innocent. What if Alice's murderer lay in wait for her further along her route home?" Yvonne broke from Tasha's hold, hurrying towards the parking area to their left.

"Where are you going?" Tasha called after her.

"To the station to view some CCTV. Are you coming?"

The DI got into her car and fired up the engine, waiting for Tasha to jump in the passenger seat.

Tasha fumbled her seatbelt into the lock. "Of course I'm

coming. I'm not letting you out on your own on a night like this."

The station was quiet and in semi-darkness, being manned only by a skeleton staff.

The DI switched on the lights in the incident room, moving straight to Ifan's desk, where he had been sorting through various discs taken from CCTV cameras. He had carefully logged and catalogued them, making it a much easier task for Yvonne to find the dates, times, and names they needed.

The footage on Alice Briefly disk was sparse, and much of that did not contain actual footage of the young woman. A shop camera had captured her for two-and-a-half seconds at one forty-seven am.

Yvonne ran the clip twice, then paused it on the best view of Alice. "So, there she is, Tasha. I think this can't have been more than fifteen minutes prior to her death. She was killed about two hundred yards up the road." She let the clip run on for a further twenty minutes on double speed.

"No-one behind." Tasha shrugged.

"No." The DI rewound the footage to twenty minutes prior to Alice appearing. Again, they watched it on double speed.

Tasha letting out the occasional yawn for which she promptly apologised.

"There." Yvonne paused the footage at a place seven minutes before the appearance of Alice. "That is the only other person we have seen within twenty minutes either side of Alice."

"A woman?"

"Yes, and we cannot see her face, unfortunately." Yvonne leaned in, peering at the screen. "But look at the size of those calves. And the shape of the back and shoulders."

"I see what you mean. Masculine-looking." She turned to the DI. "Wait, are you saying-"

"Yes. I think we are looking at a man. I believe I know who that man is."

"Who?" Tasha frowned.

"I think that's Mark Bennett. Oh, my God." Yvonne jumped up, grabbing her coat and mobile phone. "He cancelled a shift this evening. Last minute. And it wasn't because of his elderly mother."

"Wait, are you thinking he's your killer?"

"Yes. I'm putting out an APB. I will request as many officers as I can get my hands on to be on the streets of Aberystwyth tonight. He was never looking at transitioning to a female. That was his cover. Anyone asked him questions about the clothing, he could show them the consultant letters he showed to me. I'll bet that has been his reasoning all along, and it's how he got close enough to those women to lure them to their deaths. You said, yourself, he might use a disguise. Well, there it is. A drunken female will trust what she believes to be another female, late at night, far more than she would trust a male. Right?"

Tasha nodded. "Of course. We'd better find him."

∽

*He played at being drunk, priding himself on his acting. He wore only one flat-heeled shoe. The other, he'd hidden in his bag.*

*He paused, stumbled, then began frantically to search the pavement on the prom, crying and cursing in the most feminine voice he could muster. She would know he was male, but would assume he was transgender. The effect on her would be the same. She would feel relaxed. Safe. Not threatened.*

*He peered over the edge of the promenade, to the beach below. He continued doing this until she drew alongside.*

"Are you all right? Have you lost something?" There was only the slightest slur on her voice but her unsteady gait betrayed her inebriation.

*It would be easy to subdue her. Too easy.*

"I've lost my shoe. I can't find it anywhere." He slurred his words, just enough. "I think it might be down there." He pointed to the beach below them.

"I can't see it." Hannah put a hand above her eyes, as though this would help her see across the stones and sand.

"My foot is so cold." He moaned, lifting it up to give it a rub.

Hannah pulled a handkerchief from her bag and held it out to him. "It's not much, but you could tie it around your foot for extra warmth."

"Oh, you're so kind." He took the handkerchief, doing as she suggested. "I think I may have to go down on the beach and look for it."

"Good luck." Hannah said, turning away.

He called after her. "I don't suppose... I don't suppose you could help me, could you? Just for a little while?"

Hannah looked from his face, to the beach, and back the way she was heading. "I don't know, I really ought to get back." She hesitated.

"It might not take long," he pleaded.

"I don't know, I-"

"Please?"

She nodded. "Okay. Maybe for a few minutes, but then I have to go."

"Oh, you're an angel," he said, in the most effeminate voice he could muster.

## 28

## ALL HANDS ON DECK

Yvonne put out an all persons broadcast and requested that Dewi do a location check for Bennett's mobile phone. She then got DCI Llewelyn out of bed, to be the official man in charge, as his equivalent in Cardigan was still on leave.

"How sure are you that he's your killer?" Llewelyn asked, sounding less groggy than he had five minutes ago.

"Well, I think it's likely, but I have nothing more than suspicion and the circumstantial evidence of his appearing on the same CCTV camera as Alice Brierley shortly before her murder. He was dressed as a woman. I think he uses that disguise to appear less threatening to his victims. I know this may amount to nothing but, if I am right, he intends killing someone tonight. We have to prevent it. We will need a warrant for Ifan and Sarah to search Bennett's place for clothing that might match the fibres we have from the murder victims. And, honestly? This could be a significant waste of time and resources. However, if he is on the prowl, we save a life and catch a killer."

"I hope you are right, after we've mobilised everybody.

Listen, if you are out there and exposed, make sure you have adequate back-up. I'm on my way with extra officers. I'll see if we can get a chopper on standby. Keep me informed of events your end. We'll step up accordingly."

Llewelyn commandeered as many extra officers from Newtown as they could spare, along with a dog team, ordering they drive with lights and sirens all the way to the seaside town.

∼

Yvonne spoke to her sergeant on the phone. "Dewi, did you get a location for Mark Bennett's mobile?"

"Yes. And you will not like it."

"Why?"

"It was in his locker at the hospital. His manager opened it up for us. Nothing else in the locker besides spare polo shirts for work. Where are you?"

"We are on our way to the Castle, to do a sweep from the harbour through to the prom. We've got a few uniformed officers covering the town, and the DCI is on his way with backup. I'll be happier when I know where Bennett is."

"When I've finished here, should I join you?"

"I'd prefer it if you stay in the incident room, Dewi. As the central point of contact, you can help us coordinate everything. Has someone run a check on Bennett's phone, please. Find out what's on it."

"I'll do what I can."

"We will look around."

"Right-oh. Don't take risks, ma'am."

"Who me? Why would I?" She ended the call, a frown on her face.

"Are you okay?" Tasha put a hand on her arm.

"Bennett's phone was in his locker. We can't locate him that way and we have no way of knowing who his potential victim is unless there is something on his phone, which I doubt."

"Perhaps we can't find out that way, but we know that if he is planning an attack, his victim will have been drinking in a bar."

"Yes, but we simply don't have enough officers to monitor every bar in Aberystwyth."

"With any luck, the sight of several uniformed officers roaming the streets will put the wind up him and stop him starting an attack."

"That's the idea, but there are plenty of dark alleys, if he's brazen enough."

Yvonne checked her watch. Five-past eleven. "Come on. We're going to the castle. There's a good overall view of the prom from there and we are in easy reach of the harbour and Great Darkgate street. He enjoys fighting with his victims, so keep your ears and ears peeled."

## 29

## MISSING

Yvonne and Tasha reached the castle by ten-forty-five pm.

It stood, a broken but majestic edifice, bathed in an amber glow from the up-lighters strategically placed around its perimeter. They walked through and past the standing stones in the centre ground. The granite sentinels had stood there for decades, erected for the famous annual eisteddfod, a cultural festival held in various locations around Wales.

Yvonne headed through the remains of the portcullis gateway, and out onto a wooden bridge with a view of the promenade and the sea. She could barely see the beach due to the shrouding mist. Visibility was down to mere yards. The fish-tang of the sea filled their nostrils. It was stronger than usual tonight; the smell borne in by the viscous mist.

"Anything?" Tasha asked.

"No." Yvonne ran a hand through her hair. "Let's go further along, get a view of the prom."

She could see a marked police car parked at the front of

the Old College. The officers were making their way along the front, heading past the pier.

"Looks like that area is covered. Let's head to the harbour." Yvonne said, leading Tasha back the way they had come, taking the forked pathway off to the right, the route down to the harbour via Sea View Place.

The DI turned the volume up on her radio, listening for chatter that might signal a sighting of Bennett, for whom she'd given the description in the all-persons broadcast.

It was far better lit down on the street. Yvonne let out a breath, she'd been holding, as they made their way down the shadowy path from the Castle. She wasn't a fan of dark places. She wrapped her long coat tightly around her, protection from the chilling mist, chin buried in a scarf.

The harbour was quiet, save for the lapping of the water. She could see the lights of the buildings on the other side, near the harbour bridge, albeit dimmed by the vaporous air.

"All quiet this end," Tasha observed.

"Yes. I'm doubting myself. The DCI won't be impressed if I have this all wrong."

"You went with the information you-"

A voice over the airways cut Tasha off.

They stilled to listen.

"What's that? A missing girl?" Yvonne bent her head, turning the radio up further.

Tasha moved in close.

"Can you clarify? Is that a missing girl?" Yvonne asked over the radio.

"Yes, yes. IC1 female, short, dark hair, wearing jeans and a red fleece, over. Approximate height five-foot-two. Last seen in the nightclub, Why Not Bar & Lounge, approximately nine-forty-five pm. I am with two of her friends, outside the club, over."

"We'll be right there."

Shaunagh and Chloe clung to each other, fear clear in their wide eyes and tear-stained faces.

"What happened?" Yvonne asked. "Are you sure she didn't just walk home? What makes you think something happened to her?"

"Her phone is dead. It's going straight to voicemail." Shaunagh tangled her hands in her hair, her face creased with worry. "She charged it right before she left Carpenter, so it's not the battery. She leaves her phone on loud and always texts to say she's arrived back safely. She should have been home over an hour ago. We've called her neighbours in Carpenter and there is no sign of her. We wouldn't worry so much if there hadn't been... Those three girls..." Shaunagh's voice trailed off.

"I know." Yvonne put a hand on Shaunagh's shoulder. "We'll do our best to find her, I promise."

The DI called Dewi.

"Ma'am?"

"Can you ping a mobile for us?" She read Hannah's number from Shaunagh's phone. "It looks like the phone is off or out of the range of a mast. See what you can do."

"Whose phone is it?" Dewi's voice cracked on the other end as though he was fearing the worst.

"It belongs to a girl called Hannah Martin. Her friends are anxious. She was last see over an hour ago."

"Right, I'll get back to you as soon as I can. At the very least, I should be able to tell you where the phone was when it went dead."

"Brilliant. Fast as you can, Dewi."

"Okay." The sergeant hung up.

All available officers began combing the streets lining

the route from the nightclub to Carpenter Hall, calling Hannah's name as they went.

Yvonne and Tasha headed towards the promenade and the beach.

"Two of the girls ended up on the seafront." Yvonne stopped to catch her breath, looking up and down the hotels and houses on the front, before they crossed the road. "If he has her, there's a chance they will be somewhere along there."

∽

YVONNE'S MOBILE rang and vibrated in her pocket. She reached for it and saw it was the DCI. Llewelyn must have arrived with extra officers for the search.

"Hello, Yvonne?" He sounded breathless, impatient to join her.

"Yes, sir, are you here?"

"We're at the roundabout coming into Aber. Have you located the suspect?"

"Not yet, no. We have a potentially serious situation developing here, at the moment. A young woman is missing. Her friends haven't been able to get hold of her for over an hour, and she has not yet returned home. We are scouring the route she may have taken back to halls, assuming she intended going home early. Someone may have abducted her from the club."

"I will be with you in-"

"Sorry, sir, I've got Dewi on another line. He's pinging the girl's mobile phone for us. I've got to take this call."

"No problem, I'll hold."

"Dewi?"

"Ma'am, the last known location for Hannah's phone

stretches from the harbour bridge area to the beach on the other side of the coast road. We're looking at an area with a half-a-mile radius."

"Half a mile?"

"Yes. The phone was only picked up by a single mast, so triangulation is impossible. I'm sorry, that's the best I can do."

"It's okay, you've done well, Dewi. Llewelyn is on his way with reinforcements. I'll get them to comb the area with us. Tasha and I are heading there now. I'll let Llewelyn know where to go, he is on hold. I hope we get to her on time. If he has her, she won't have long."

"Good luck, ma'am."

"Thanks."

## 30

## DESPERATION

Hannah was sobering up. Becoming more aware of her surroundings. Perhaps it was the breeze coming off the sea that cleared her head. The same breeze that had transported the mist through the Aberystwyth streets.

"Have you seen anything?" Her companion asked.

Hannah shot him a glance. "No. You?"

"Yes."

"Have you got it?" She hoped so, she needed her bed.

He lunged for her, grabbing her around the waist and spinning her such that her back was to him. "I've got you." He placed a large hand over her mouth. The arm around her waist squeezed the air from her lungs. She gasped, her eyes wide with shock.

More than a foot smaller than her attacker, fighting back was difficult. She tried stamping on his instep and elbowing him in the ribs. It was then she noticed that he was wearing both shoes. He hadn't lost one at all. She couldn't believe she had fallen for such an obvious ploy. Her elbow missed his side and the stamp to his instep barely connected.

He forced her right arm up her back and she thought it might break as intense pain shot through her shoulder and collarbone.

She tried screaming but strong fingers muffled the sound and squeezed her jaw in painful punishment.

He marched her along the shore at South Beach, heading toward Tanybwlch and further away from lights, life, and any hope of rescue. She had wondered why he wore flat shoes with that dress. Now, she had her answer. He'd been prowling for prey. He'd found her.

Hannah's legs shook and tears rolled down her face as she realised she was probably in the grip of the Seaside strangler, the name given to the killer by a story-hungry press. Ironic that she should be a victim, given she had been the one telling her friends not to walk home alone.

∼

"Can you see anything?" Tasha called to Yvonne, as they ran across the road from the Old College towards the beach.

"No, it's pretty murky down there," the DI answered, panting.

They reached the pavement and glanced both ways along the beach for as far as they could see, their field of view still limited by the viscosity of the mist.

"Wait." Yvonne held a hand up. "I hear something."

Tasha stilled to listen with her. It sounded like a muffled cry coming from somewhere below.

The DI ran ahead, stopping at the first convenient place to jump down from the wall onto the stoney beach. She stumbled but quickly regained her footing, searching the murk for the person who had tried calling out.

The psychologist caught up with her and they stopped to listen for further cries. All they could hear was the sea.

"I think it was coming from along there." Yvonne pointed ahead, and they continued picking their way through the stones and rock pools.

What they heard next was unmistakable. A struggle, happening ahead.

Out of the gloom, two figures emerged. It looked like a large woman and a young boy.

As they drew closer, Yvonne recognised Mark Bennett with a short-haired young woman who was trying to fend him off."

"Stop, police!" The DI shouted, holding her hand up.

Bennett pulled Hannah against him, such that she was facing forward, with his hand over her mouth. With his other hand, he pulled out a knife from his bag, putting it to the young woman's throat.

"Don't come any closer," he warned through gritted teeth. "I swear, I'll kill her."

Yvonne stopped in her tracks, still with her hands up. "Okay, okay. Don't do anything stupid, Mark. We won't come any closer, all right?"

"I will kill her," he stated, again.

Yvonne drew close to Tasha. "Talk to him. Keep him calm. I will back off a bit and let the DCI know where we are, so he can get people down here."

"Yes, of course." Tasha took a step towards Bennet and the girl.

"I said don't come any closer." Mark pushed the knife up under the young woman's chin."

"All right, all right. Look, I will stay right here, Okay? I won't move from this spot. I want you to stay calm and not do anything silly. I want you and the young lady to relax. I don't want either of you harmed."

Overhead, Tasha could hear a helicopter. Its search light scoured the surrounding murk.

The psychologist groaned, mentally willing the pilot to back off. It was difficult enough to hear what Bennett was saying. With the chopper overhead, it would be impossible.

Yvonne came back to her shoulder. "The DCI will be here in minutes," she shouted in Tasha's ear.

"Get him to call the chopper off."

"What?"

Tasha put her mouth to Yvonne's ear. "Get him to call off the police helicopter. We can't talk to Bennett with that thing overhead."

"Right. Got you." The DI ran back to make the call.

"Mark? Mark, can you hear me?" Tasha turned her attention to Bennett and his hostage. "I don't want anying bad to happen to you. Why don't you let the girl go?"

It was useless. She couldn't make herself heard and would have to wait until the helicopter had gone.

Bennett looked about him, as though weighing up whether to make a dash for it.

Moments later and the helicopter moved further inland.

They could still hear it, but only just.

Tasha tried again. "Mark, why don't you let the Hannah go? You can't go anywhere and she is frightened. Let her go."

She saw the confusion in his face.

"It's all right. Just let her go."

He threw the girl down on the floor, and set off running down the beach, knife still in hand.

"Damn it." Yvonne, who had finished her call to the DCI, set off after him.

"Yvonne? Wait for backup." Tasha called after her. She needn't have bothered. The DI was on a mission.

Tasha ran to Hannah to check her over, just as the DCI and the other officers arrived with lights and sirens.

The psychologist pointed in the direction Yvonne and Bennett had gone. "He's armed with a knife," she shouted.

"What?" the DCI ran towards her.

The chopper was back.

"Bennett's got a knife. Yvonne has gone after him."

"Right." Llewelyn barked instructions into his radio.

## 31

## LIFE OR DEATH

Yvonne caught up with Bennett just before he reached the breakwater.

He turned round, swiping the knife at her.

She stood about five feet away, arms out, watching the knife. "Mark, we can end this now. Drop the weapon on the floor."

He lunged forward, swiping at her again.

She jumped back. "Listen, Mark, armed officers will be here any moment. You have nowhere to go. If they see you trying to slash me, they will shoot you dead. Is that what you want?"

"It doesn't matter now, does it? They'll either kill me or I'll spend the rest of my life in prison. I'm dead either way."

"It doesn't have to end like this, Mark."

"Yeah, it does."

"What about your mother?"

"Leave my mother out of this."

"You love her, don't you?"

"I said, leave her out of it." His face twisted, betraying an inner agony.

"Who'll look out for her if you go?"

Shouts went up from behind her.

"You hear that, Mark? They are the armed officers I told you about. They're excited. They get the chance to put into practice all that target shooting they've been doing. Are you going to let them have the satisfaction of taking you down? Are you going to give them that?"

The arm holding the knife dropped to his side, though he continued to hold on to the weapon.

His indecision was palpable.

She was close. She knew it. "Listen, even if you're in prison, you can still call your mum. You can still speak to the home and have an input into your mum's care. And you can get help for those demons."

"I don't need help. There isn't any help for me." The knife arm stretched out once more. "Do you think they can just put me back together again? Do you think they can talk me into changing? Not even you are that stupid, surely? I enjoyed what I did. How are they going to stop that, eh?"

"You don't know what's possible if you don't try."

He took another swipe.

"Don't do this, please. It's over."

"When did you know it was me?" he asked, waving the knife around.

"I put it together, when Stephen Yates denied being your partner, and the hospital doubted your commitment to changing genders. Oh, and I saw you on CCTV, the night you killed Alice Brierley. You didn't follow them, did you? You were always in front or lying in wait."

He lunged at her with the knife. "I'd get out of the way if I was you."

Yvonne backed off further. "If I move aside now, they will shoot you. Please put the knife down."

He stood motionless.

"Mark, I won't move if you put the knife down. I'll stay right here. They won't shoot you while I'm standing in front of you. Please, put the knife down."

∿

THE CHOPPER FLEW OVER, search lights fixed on the two of them.

Bennett looked up at it.

"Don't shoot." Yvonne stared up too, willing the occupants not to do anything rash. "Please, I'm almost there."

When she looked back, Bennett was off and running again. "Oh, for goodness' sake. Mark, don't run, they'll shoot."

She called the DCI on her mobile, as she ran after Bennett. "Call the chopper off, please. He was responding to me. I think I can talk him into giving up."

"I'm behind you." Llewelyn informed her.

She turned around to see him less than fifty yards behind. She continued chasing Bennet. The killer was running out of beach as officers flooded in from the left.

He stopped running, bent over double from the effort, trying to regain his breath. Bennett was spent.

Yvonne caught up, grabbing him while he was in that state, surprised at the utter lack of resistance. He was limp. So much so, she could easily slip the knife from his grasp.

She pushed the back of his knee with her right foot and, as he fell to his knees in the sand, she cuffed him from behind, double locking the rigid cuffs.

She jumped when the DCI placed a hand on her arm. "Jesus!"

"Hey, It's me. You knew I was behind, didn't you?"

She grimaced. "You'd be jumpy if you'd just been through everything I have."

"Come on." He moved forward to commandeer Bennett as other the officers surrounded them in case the prisoner kicked off. "Let's take him in."

## 32

## AFTERMATH

The following morning, Yvonne caught up with her team for the final debrief.

Ifan and Sarah had located clothing in Bennett's flat that were potential matches for the fibres on the dead girls. These had been carefully gathered, and the DI went through everything to check it was properly bagged and tagged. It wouldn't do for Bennett to get off on a technicality. They owed the victims and their families justice and she was determined that would get it.

Tasha joined her, bearing coffees. "You know how to scare me witless, don't you?"

Yvonne chuckled. "How else could you be sure it was me?"

"Can't you change jobs to something more sedate? Flower arranging, perhaps?"

"Were you terrified?" The DI grinned.

"Yes, I never know what you will do next. I only know that you seem to be a magnet for danger and run headlong into it like a headless lemming."

Yvonne laughed. "A headless lemming? Is that even a thing?"

"There you are." Dewi joined them. "Ooh, coffee. Is there one for me?"

Tasha nodded. "I brought a tray, help yourself."

"Hey, you two," Yvonne called to Sarah and Ifan, who were sorting through paperwork. "Come and get a coffee." And, as they joined her, she added, "Thank you for all your help on this case. It was an excellent team effort."

"Thank you." Ifan grabbed himself a drink. "I've learned a lot from this investigation, and from you."

She nodded. "Good. You and Sarah have a bright future ahead of you. You are excellent officers."

The DCI came in, the bags under his eyes, and his unkempt hair, suggested he'd had a sleepless night. "Right, I'm off back to Newtown. Yvonne, Dewi, Tasha, any of you need a lift?"

They shook their heads.

"We've still got stuff to wrap up here, sir." Yvonne explained. "We'll see you later."

"As you like. You all did a great job well done." He yawned. "Yvonne, we'll talk when you get back."

"Drive safe. You look tired." She advised.

He waved a hand behind him as he headed through the door without looking back.

∽

THE MORNING WAS crisp and clear in the piercing sunlight, in contrast to the damp mist of the previous night. Hoar frost covered the trees, grass and shrubs. Frozen leaves crunched under her feet.

Yvonne took the car keys from her pocket and pressed to unlock it.

The DI and Tasha were the last to leave the station, as Yvonne had stayed behind to finish the last of the paperwork.

Tasha used the ladies' room before the drive back. The DI ambled slowly to the car.

Across the road, a middle-aged woman pushed her sunglasses up onto her head and peered at her.

Yvonne cast a glance behind, to see if the woman was looking at someone else. She wasn't.

"Are you okay?" She asked, as the woman approached. She noted the long, greying hair, held back in a ponytail. The woman had her hands pushed deep inside the pockets of her long, woollen coat.

"Are you DI Giles? DI Yvonne Giles?"

Yvonne squinted in the bright sunlight. "Yes, I am."

"Hi, my name is Sheila Winters."

"What can I do for you?" The DI's gut tightened uncomfortably. It was something about the other-worldliness of the woman's stare. It disconcerted her. Like the woman was seeing her but not seeing her. Looking through her.

"I've heard you are one of the best at solving cases and finding murderers." The woman stopped just in front of Yvonne, blocking her path.

Behind her, the DI could hear the door of the station opening and closing. Thank God, Tasha was coming. "I don't know about being the best Mrs Winters but, yes, I have caught a few murderers in my time. What's wrong? Do you need help?"

The woman nodded, her face, gaunt. Haunted. Half-shadowed, by the morning sun.

"Mrs Winters?" Yvonne asked again, as the woman gazed past her with a thousand-yard stare.

"Is everything all right?" Tasha was at the DI's shoulder.

Yvonne shrugged. "I don't know." She tilted her head to peer at the lady. "Mrs Winters?" she said with increased volume.

The woman jumped. "Yes. Sorry."

"You were about to tell me something?" Yvonne frowned, confused about what was going on with the woman. "Has there been a murder?"

"Yes. I think so."

The DI scratched her head. "You think?"

"Sorry, I know I'm not making much sense."

"What's happened?" Yvonne asked with greater urgency. She wanted to give Sheila Winters a shake.

She didn't.

"I think I murdered someone." Sheila turned piercing blue eyes to her. There was intelligence in them. And pain.

Yvonne was still.

Sheila continued. "I think I murdered someone thirty years ago, when I was twenty years old. I killed another young woman. I don't know who, I don't know where, and I don't know why…"

# AFTERWORD

**Mailing list:** You can join my emailing list here : AnnamarieMorgan.com

**Facebook page:** AnnamarieMorganAuthor

**You might also like to read the other books in the series:**
　**Book 1: Death Master:**
　After months of mental and physical therapy, Yvonne Giles, an Oxford DI, is back at work and that's just how she likes it. So when she's asked to hunt the serial killer responsible for taking apart young women, the DI jumps at the chance but hides the fact she is suffering debilitating flashbacks. She is told to work with Tasha Phillips, an in-her-face, criminal psychologist. The DI is not enamoured with the idea. Tasha has a lot to prove. Yvonne has a lot to get over. A tentative link with a 20 year-old cold case brings them closer to the truth but events then take a horrifyingly personal turn.

**Book 2: You Will Die**

After apprehending an Oxford Serial Killer, and almost losing her life in the process, DI Yvonne Giles has left England for a quieter life in rural Wales.Her peace is shattered when she is asked to hunt a priest-killing psychopath, who taunts the police with messages inscribed on the corpses.Yvonne requests the help of Dr. Tasha Phillips, a psychologist and friend, to aid in the hunt. But the killer is one step ahead and the ultimatum, he sets them, could leave everyone devastated.

### Book 3: Total Wipeout

A whole family is wiped out with a shotgun. At first glance, it's an open-and-shut case. The dad did it, then killed himself. The deaths follow at least two similar family wipeouts – attributed to the financial crash.

So why doesn't that sit right with Detective Inspector Yvonne Giles? And why has a rape occurred in the area, in the weeks preceding each family's demise? Her seniors do not believe there are questions to answer. DI Giles must therefore risk everything, in a high-stakes investigation ofa mysterious masonic ring and players in high finance.

Can she find the answers, before the next innocent family is wiped out?

### Book 4: Deep Cut

In a tiny hamlet in North Wales, a female recruit is murdered whilst on Christmas home leave. Detective Inspector Yvonne Giles is asked to cut short her own leave, to investigate. Why was the young soldier killed? And is her death related to several alleged suicides at her army base? DI Giles this it is, and that someone powerful has a dark secret they will do anything to hide.

### Book 5: The Pusher

Young men are turning up dead on the banks of the River Severn. Some of them have been missing for days or even weeks. The only thing the police can be sure of, is that the men have drowned. Rumours abound that a mythical serial killer has turned his attention from the Manchester canal to the waterways of Mid-Wales. And now one of CID's own is missing. A brand new recruit with everything to live for. DI Giles must find him before it's too late.

### Book 6: Gone

Children are going missing. They are not heard from again until sinister requests for cryptocurrency go viral. The public must pay or the children die. For lead detective Yvonne Giles, the case is complicated enough. And then the unthinkable happens...

### Book 7: Bone Dancer

A serial killer is murdering women, threading their bones back together, and leaving them for police to find. Detective Inspector Yvonne Giles must find him before more innocent victims die. Problem is, the killer wants her and will do anything he can to get her. Unaware that she, herself, is is a target, DI Giles risks everything to catch him.

### Book 8: Blood Lost

A young man comes home to find his whole family missing. Half-eaten breakfasts and blood spatter on the lounge wall are the only clues to what happened...

### Book 9: Angel of Death

*He is watching. Biding his time. Preparing himself for a*

*torturous kill. Soaring above; lord of all. His journey, direct through the lives of the unsuspecting.*

*The Angel of Death is nigh.*

The peace of the Mid-Wales countryside is shattered, when a female eco-warrior is found crucified in a public wood. At first, it would appear a simple case of finding which of the woman's enemies had had her killed. But DI Yvonne Giles has no idea how bad things are going to get. As the body count rises, she will need all of her instincts, and the skills of those closest to her, to stop the murderous rampage of the Angel of Death.

**Book 10: Death in the Mist**

The morning after a viscous sea-mist covers the seaside town of Aberystwyth, a young student lies brutalised within one hundred yards of the castle ruins.

DI Yvonne Giles' reputation precedes her. Having successfully captured more serial killers than some detectives have caught colds, she is seconded to head the murder investigation team, and hunt down the young woman's killer.

What she doesn't know, is this is only the beginning...

Printed in Poland
by Amazon Fulfillment
Poland Sp. z o.o., Wrocław